Labyrinth Junction

Hayley Davenport-Smith

Matador
9 Priory Business Park,
Wistow Road, Kibworth Beauchamp,
Leicestershire. LE8 0RX
Tel: 0116 279 2299
Email: books@troubador.co.uk
Web: www.troubador.co.uk/matador
Twitter: @matadorbooks

ISBN 978 1789017 021

British Library Cataloguing in Publication Data.
A catalogue record for this book is available from the British Library.

Printed and bound in Great Britain by 4edge Limited
Typeset in 12pt Minion Pro by Troubador Publishing Ltd, Leicester, UK

Matador is an imprint of Troubador Publishing Ltd

In loving memory of my dad and hero,
Ian Gerald Davenport.

Contents

Chapter 1

Labyrinth Junction

Ben's heart pounded in his chest as he ran, and he gasped for breath. Little did he realise, that within the next few minutes, his life would no longer resemble normality as he knew it.

"I'm catching you up, Ben!" bellowed Jacob, one of the cruel boys chasing him. "Don't think you are going to get away."

Ben knew that he had made a mistake fleeing in this direction, but he carried on running, eager to escape the two bullies. A lock of dark hair fell in front of his big green eyes and he quickly swept it away with his hand as he fled. Panic swept over him as he realised he would soon reach the shoreline, where the land ended and the sea began. It was far too cold to jump into the sea, and besides, Ben wasn't a very confident swimmer. He needed to think quickly and find somewhere safe to hide.

His stomach knotted as he reached the edge of the shingle beach. That's when he remembered the cave entrance, high up in the cliff, away to the right where the rocky headland jutted out into the sea. He had always wondered what was in the cave, but his mother would never let him climb up to look; she had told him that it was far too dangerous.

"Where are you going to run now, Ben?" echoed Owen's sarcastic tones in the distance.

Ben decided that there was no other option but to try and scramble up to the strange, dark cave. They probably wouldn't follow him up there; surely they would be too scared!

He quickly reached the bottom of the steep cliff and began to climb. He felt uneasy as he found a few small ledges for footholds and steadily began to haul himself up. He was ascending quite quickly, and when he looked down, he realised that he was already fairly high above the ground. The two callous boys had reached the bottom of the cliff face, and to Ben's dismay, they also started to climb. He hastily found another ledge and tried to pull himself up further, but the rock face was cold and slippery and it felt sharp beneath his fingertips. Fear engulfed him as he lost his footing, and for a moment he thought he was going to lose his grip and fall, but by some small miracle he managed to hang on and save himself from tumbling.

Finally, his hand touched the wide ledge of the cave opening. He took a deep breath, and with all the strength he could muster, pulled himself up. Relief swept over him as he sat on the ledge, and with renewed confidence he dared to peer below. It looked a very long way down, and he could see the beach and the grey sea crashing against the rocks in the distance. He could hear the boys' voices and he leaned a little further over the edge of the cliff, his green eyes searching for them below. He hoped they would have given up by now, but his heart sank as he realised they were still in pursuit.

Eager to escape, Ben stared into the dark and gloomy cave and slowly crept inside. He couldn't tell how far back it went as he walked deeper into the shadows. He slowed as the cave narrowed, and realised he could now touch both walls with his arms outstretched. He was in almost complete darkness and the cave felt cold, damp and eerie. Ben wondered whether he should wait until the boys had gone, and he stood still and listened. At first there was only silence, but then he heard the muffled sounds of Owen and Jacob's voices and realised they had reached the small, rugged entrance. Ben felt an air of nervousness as he decided to continue on his perilous journey. The cave narrowed even further, and he began to squeeze himself between the walls into the gloom.

Eventually, he saw a faint glow of light in the distance. At first he thought that it was his imagination playing tricks on him, so he stood still to focus his eyes… yes, it was definitely light ahead. He continued moving forward and to his amazement, came to a flight of rocky steps with a beam of light shining down brightly from above. He felt uneasy as he slowly climbed them, not knowing what he would encounter when he reached the top.

But to his astonishment, he found himself entering a strange, circular, dome-shaped room. The light was coming from a fire in the middle, and beside the flames sat an old, wrinkled woman with long, matted grey hair and a large hooked nose. Ben gasped in bewilderment at the strange sight. She looked very much like a witch in her long, black cloak! Over the fire was an enormous black pot, and she was stirring something inside it. The old woman was much larger than Ben, and he briefly wondered how she could have got here, through the tiny, narrow passageway… unless there was another way in, perhaps?

"Welcome to Labyrinth Junction," croaked the old witch.

"Welcome to where?" Ben stuttered, astoundment in his voice.

"Labyrinth Junction, of course!" snapped the hag. "Can't you read the sign?"

Ben looked up and saw a large, red sign on the cavern wall, bearing the words *LABYRINTH JUNCTION.*

"About time someone passed through… I've been waiting here all day!" she grumbled as she studied Ben intently.

"Waiting for whom?" he replied nervously, pushing his dark hair away from his eyes to get a closer look at the strange sight before him.

"For a passer-by, of course!"

"I'm not a passer-by," protested Ben. "I was just trying to run away from some horrible boys."

"People give me all sorts of excuses in here," declared

the witch. "Now, which way do you want to go?"

"Excuse me?"

"Which way do you want to go?" she snapped impatiently, as if it was a very simple question. "Come on, I haven't got all day, you know!"

"Which way can I go?" Ben replied sharply, starting to feel a little irritated at being spoken to in such a rude manner.

"Well, if you don't know where you are going, I can't understand why you are here," she said brusquely. "Have a look and see!"

Ben looked around the room and saw lots of equations and formulae written on the walls: $e = mc^2$; $pi = \pi = 3.1415926$; $A = \pi r^2$; $a = 2b + 3c$.

"Why are there lots of numbers and mathematical signs on the walls?"

"Don't they teach you anything at school, laddie?" she snapped. "Mathematics, numbers, equations, physics… they solve many of the world's problems, but people are just too ignorant to see it. You will learn that on your travels. Regard that as a bit of important advice for your impending journey! Now, which way are you going?"

Ben continued to look around the cavern. He noticed that there were four narrow passageways leading off the room. They had the letters N, E, S, and W marked above them.

"Hurry up!" said the witch. "There are four passageways to choose from – that's presuming you don't want to go back the way you came?"

"What do the letters stand for?" asked Ben in a confused manner.

"As I said, they don't teach children anything worthwhile at school nowadays!" the old woman cackled.

Ben quickly realised the letters were positioned at opposite sides of the circular cave. He pointed at each entrance as he spoke. "They mean north, east, south, and west. They are all geographical directions, like on a compass," he said eagerly, feeling very pleased with himself that he had worked out what the letters stood for.

"Don't be ridiculous!" snapped the witch. She picked up a small piece of paper and handed it to Ben. "I presume school taught you how to read?" she asked sarcastically.

Ben studied the piece of paper and read aloud:

N = Numblebrook
E = Eggington Edge
S = Smugglers' Way
W = Wigglesworm

He could hear Owen and Jacob's voices echoing from within the dark passage and realised that they must be getting close. He needed to make up his mind quickly!

"I'll go to Numblebrook!" said Ben without hesitation, picking the first place on the list.

"That will be ten noggings," the old hag stated abruptly.

"What are noggings?"

"Money, obviously!" she shrieked.

"But I don't have any noggings!" protested Ben.

"Well then, you won't be able to pass, will you? That is, unless you want to run an errand and earn your passage?"

"What errand would that be?"

She removed a bright green envelope from under her long, black cloak. "You can deliver this to Haligan Lexin for me," she replied, in a very matter-of-fact way.

"Who's Haligan Lexin?"

"You can find that out for yourself. Now, do you want to deliver it or not? If not, you can't pass. You can't come and go as you please through here, you know!"

"OK, I'll try," mumbled Ben anxiously, eager to avoid any encounter with Owen and Jacob.

The witch handed him the green envelope and he placed it neatly in his pocket.

"Remember to look after it carefully," she advised. "The dog will take you through the passageway."

A small, sandy-coloured dog with huge droopy ears appeared from under the witch's long, black cloak. Ben hadn't noticed it before, and stared at it in surprise. It seemed to know what had been discussed and started to amble towards the passageway with the letter *N* above the entrance.

"Just a second – before you go, you had better take these; I've got a feeling you might be needing them! I only made them this morning, so they are very fresh." The witch handed him a jar full of small red balls.

"What are they?"

"Sweets. I suggest you eat one if you find yourself in trouble. But a word of warning: use them wisely! They don't work near heat and only Giddles should eat them; they don't work on anyone else. That's the second bit of advice I've given you already! Take heed, boy. I'm not usually this forthcoming! You must have caught me in a good mood today."

"Who are Giddles?" Ben asked, whilst wondering what on earth she would have been like if he had encountered her in a bad mood!

"Earthling children like yourself, of course! Now hurry along, the dog is waiting."

Ben wanted to ask some more questions about the red sweets, but thought better of it. He put the jar in his coat pocket and turned to follow the strange dog. To his astonishment, he noticed that the dog had two tails which drooped towards the floor and swayed in a very peculiar fashion as it strolled along the passage. He thought about asking why this was, but again decided against any more questions. Besides, he wanted to leave quickly, before Owen and Jacob arrived and caused him more trouble!

The dog led him through the passageway and, like the one Ben had come through before, it was dark, damp and narrow. A feeling of both excitement and fear stirred in the pit of his stomach as he shuffled slowly through the tunnel towards the light in the distance.

After a few hundred yards, the dog turned to him.

"This is where I will leave you!" it announced knowingly.

Ben staggered backwards in surprise. A talking dog… things were getting stranger by the minute!

"OK, thanks," he managed to reply in utter disbelief as he stared at the peculiar canine.

He stepped out of the passageway and found himself standing on a grassy slope, high up on a hillside. He gasped in awe at the magnificent and colourful scenery before him. The grass sloped sharply downwards towards a wood, and there appeared to be a ravine in the valley beyond. He looked ahead and saw huge mounds of rock and grass floating in the deep-blue sky. They were like islands you would normally see out at sea, but they were just hanging in the air. He saw something fly into the sky from one of the floating islands, and thought it looked distinctly like a dragon. He knew he was no longer in the world that he recognised as his own. This world was beautiful and serene, but so very different. He felt a nervous chill run down his spine as he realised he was a long way from home.

All of a sudden, he heard rumbling in the distance and a pretty girl with flowing bright blonde hair came running down the slope towards him. As she was about to run past, she stopped and looked at him worriedly.

"Don't just stand there!" she gasped. "Run quickly… the King is coming!"

"What king?"

"King Ados, of course!" shouted the girl. "Run and hide quickly. If he sees you, he will lock you in Numblebrook Island Prison!"

Ben could detect the fear in her voice, and he looked up the slope in the direction of the rumbling sound. Just coming into view over the summit of the hill was a procession of pure-white horses, ridden by men holding long poles. From each pole flew a large triangular flag bearing a coat of arms. As they came into view, Ben could see that many of the men were very small – tiny, in fact. They looked similar to dwarfs, but they each had a small, pointed horn protruding from their forehead and their claw-like hands gripped long, sharp spears. However, the man at the front was certainly no small, strange horned creature. He appeared very tall, with long, wavy blond hair. He wore a majestic crown and a golden cloak flowed from his shoulders. Although he was a handsome man, Ben knew immediately that evil flowed through his bones, for suddenly he was filled with terror, paralysing him.

The blonde girl had hurried off into the trees in the distance and there was nowhere nearby to hide. Ben didn't want to be caught and imprisoned, and decided he would rather risk bumping into Owen and Jacob. A nerve quickened in his throat as he hastily turned to escape back down the passageway through which he had entered this mysterious and peculiar land. But to his horror, there was only open grassland behind him. The passageway was nowhere to be seen… it had simply disappeared!

Chapter 2
The Magic Sweets

Fear splintered Ben's heart as he stood in bewilderment, finding it difficult to comprehend why the passage was no longer there. He knew that it should be just behind him, less than a few feet away… but it had completely vanished and was nowhere to be seen. Behind him the land sloped upwards and there was nothing but green, flowing grass waving gently in the wind.

The King was advancing quickly towards him, and Ben remembered the girl's warning. She had fled towards the trees and was now out of sight. Fear clawed through him as he began running down the hillside in the direction of the wood, but he was too late; the men and their horses were galloping at speed towards him. The King reined his horse to a stop and stared at Ben in disbelief. A small horned creature blasted a trumpet, and the deafening sound it produced could be heard for miles around.

"By the order of King Ados, I demand you stop!" bellowed a voice.

A chill shuddered through Ben's body as he came to a standstill and turned to look at the procession of horses and men. The King was a good-looking man, but Ben knew by the evil look in his eyes that he was one to be feared. A haze of golden, shimmering light surrounded the blade of his sword, and Ben knew immediately that this was no ordinary weapon.

"He looks like a Giddle to me!" said a cruel, ugly-looking fellow.

"Seize him!" bellowed the King.

Immediately the horned dwarf-like creatures pointed their spears and started galloping towards Ben. His heart was in his throat as he turned to flee, but he quickly realised he had no chance of escape. Then he remembered the red sweets in his pocket, the ones the old hag had given him. A vision of her appeared in his mind, and he recalled her words.

"*I suggest you eat one if you find yourself in trouble. But a word of warning: use them wisely*," she had told him.

He stopped and quickly pulled the jar from his pocket. He unscrewed the lid and removed what looked like a tiny, shiny red sweet. Ben didn't have time to examine it in any detail and popped the sweet into his mouth whilst he ran. It tasted like strawberries and ice cream, with a hint of raspberry and meringue, and it just seemed to melt in his mouth. Ben was wondering what it was supposed to do, when his hands began to tingle and the feeling started to spread through his entire body. He lifted his arm up in front of him and stared at his hand in utter wonderment; it was slowly becoming transparent. The image of his arm before him became hazier until it vanished altogether. Ben stopped in his tracks... he could no longer see his arms or legs; in fact, he could not see any part of his body at all. He and all his attire had become completely invisible. Hope fluttered inside him as he realised this was his greatest chance of escape!

"Where's he gone?" shouted a deep voice from behind. The odd-looking creatures rode around, looking frantic and confused.

"He just disappeared!" shouted another.

The King galloped down the hillside behind them. "What happened?" he screeched angrily. "You can't possibly have let him escape, you imbeciles!"

"He just disappeared!" repeated one of the horned beings. "One minute he was running down the hill and the next minute he just vanished, Your Highness!"

"A Giddle who uses magic?!" screamed the King. "I will not allow it. I don't care how long it takes; he must be found!"

King Ados turned his horse to go back in the direction from which he had come. "When he is found I want him brought to the palace immediately!" he shrieked angrily.

He rode off into the distance with the tall, ugly guard, who Ben presumed was probably his right-hand man. The weird creatures gathered together, looking angry and stern, and Ben could hear them muttering. He used the opportunity to flee towards the woods; the quicker he escaped from them, the better. Besides, he didn't know how long the magic sweet's effect would last and how soon he would be visible again.

The creatures finished their frantic discussion and rode off in various directions, searching for him. To Ben's relief, he eventually made it to the edge of the wood and rested on a fallen tree until they were completely out of sight.

Whilst he sat, he thought about his family and wondered if he would ever see them again. His mother would surely be wondering where he was by now. He had gone out to play and she had told him to be back by lunchtime. Ben realised he shouldn't have run down to the beach, but when he had bumped into Owen and Jacob and they had started calling him names, he had panicked. Jacob was a mean individual with a huge ego. He would manipulate Owen in a sneaky way to serve his evil antics, which wasn't difficult when Owen was far too gullible! Ben didn't believe Owen was a nasty child, just easily led and a little silly.

He thought about how much trouble he would be in when he got home for disobeying his mother. His two older brothers were allowed to go wherever they pleased and had lots of friends, but Ben was forever being told he was too young to be out all day on his own. He also had two little sisters, and they always seemed to get lots of attention because they were young and pretty. Ben blamed everything on being a middle child! He was only twelve years old, but often came across as wise for his years… not in a nerdy kind of way, but in the way he expressed himself and judged grown-up situations. He was of average height for a twelve-year-old, with dark auburn hair and beautiful big green eyes. He was a good-natured, sociable boy who was often told he talked far too much, but despite this he was an excellent scholar who always aimed to please. His dad's job had recently changed, and the family had relocated to the coast from the city. His brothers and sisters had settled well, but Ben had struggled to make friends. A lot of the other boys in the class kept calling him 'the new boy' and belittling him; Ben wasn't sure whether it was because he was more intelligent than the average twelve-year-old or because he talked too much. He had thought about telling his mother, but felt embarrassed and thought that she might go storming into school to speak to the head teacher. That would only make matters worse!

As Ben sat pondering, he suddenly felt the tingling sensation return to his fingers. It spread up his arms and legs and then through his whole body. After a few more seconds the tingling stopped and he realised he was visible again. Ben wasn't sure whether this was a good or bad thing, but he did feel a sense of relief that the sweets hadn't made him permanently invisible.

"How did you do that?" asked a voice from behind him. Ben swung around and saw the blonde girl standing in the trees a few feet away. Her bright blue eyes studied him with caution.

"Where were you hiding?"

"I came to lie low in the wood," said the girl gently, as she flicked her long, tousled hair behind her shoulder. "I know all the secret hiding places around here. You haven't answered my question... how did you do that? You just disappeared!"

"An old hag gave me some magic sweets," said Ben proudly. "I think she was a witch!"

"There's no such thing as witches!"

"I saw her with my own eyes!" Ben insisted.

"Prove it... give me a magic sweet and I'll see if it makes me invisible too!"

"The witch told me that they only work on Giddles. Are you a Giddle?" asked Ben.

"Oh no, I'm not a Giddle. I've heard of them, but I've never actually seen one. I heard that Giddles are children from Earthlingcragg. Are you from Earthlingcragg?"

"Well, I must be," said Ben. "The witch told me
I'm a Giddle."

"Well, you certainly don't look like you are from
around here," added the girl as she studied him in
detail. "You have brown hair and green eyes."

"Don't people have brown hair and green eyes
here?" asked Ben curiously.

"No," stated the girl softly, "not people, anyway.
All the people have blonde hair and blue eyes like me.

Some of the Unicerons have dark hair, but not the people."

"What are Unicerons?"

"Unicerons are those funny-looking small beings with horns on their heads. We call them Unicerons because they remind us of weird unicorn-type creatures. Everyone knows unicorns don't exist, but Unicerons do! Beware of them… they support the King and they are our enemies! Anyway, how did you get here?"

"I came through Labyrinth Junction!"

The girl stared at him with an amazed look on her pretty face. "Labyrinth Junction? Do you mean it's near here? People have been searching for Labyrinth Junction for years!"

"I came out of the passageway just up the hillside, the place where you ran past me, but when I turned to go back down it had disappeared!"

"I've never seen Labyrinth Junction," chirped the girl, "but I've heard the tales about it. It's supposed to be a gateway to other worlds, but people say it never stays in the same place for too long. King Ados and his men have been looking for it for years. They want to make sure it is destroyed so that nobody can enter or leave our land. If anyone sees it, they are to report it to the King immediately!"

"I need to find it!" declared Ben anxiously. "I want to go home. My mother will be wondering where I am… she'll be worried."

"Well, I'm afraid I cannot help you," answered the girl sadly.

Ben looked at her glumly. "Why were you running away from the King?"

"Because this is his property and we are trespassing on his land. I often come here to play in the woods, but anyone who is found will be punished and locked away on Numblebrook Island Prison. King Ados isn't a very nice king; he's wicked and mean. The people here don't like him, but they are too scared to do anything about it. If he finds you he will imprison you immediately; he detests Giddles."

"What's Numblebrook Island Prison? It sounds scary!" Ben asked apprehensively.

"It's a prison on one of the islands in the sky. It's a miserable place where people are used as slaves. They cannot escape as there is nowhere to go, unless they jump off the island that is, but it's so high up they would never survive. King Ados imprisons anyone who dares to disobey him, that's if he doesn't kill them first."

"The sword in his hand had a glowing light around it!"

"That's the Sword of Gwyntog. It's a magic sword. In the wrong hands it can cause great harm. It used to belong to the Moonbeamers when they ruled the land and they used its power wisely, but King Ados uses it to cause nothing but death and destruction."

Ben shuddered at the thought.

"I'm Amy, by the way. What's your name? I've never met a Giddle before. To be honest, I wasn't sure they even existed!" Amy held out her hand.

"My name's Benjamin, but people call me Ben."

"Benjamin Giddle, that's what I will call you," she laughed.

Ben liked Amy immediately. She looked to be around the same age as himself, and was an attractive girl with a huge smile and kind, crystal-blue eyes. She seemed forthright and outspoken, but an honest and likeable type. Although Ben had only just met her, his instincts told him that she would make a genuine and loyal friend who could be trusted.

"I must find my way home. Do you know anyone who could help me?" he pleaded.

"Maybe I could take you to the Citadel."

"What's the Citadel?"

"It's where the Moonbeamers live. They are the true kings of this land, but evil King Ados' father stole the crown from them. They were kind and fair and ruled the land well. When King Ados' father stole the crown, the Moonbeamers were banished to the Citadel. They were told they could live there in peace as long as they did not try to take back the realm. Some say they still possess some of their old magic. They might know where to find Labyrinth Junction… follow me, I'll take you there!"

Ben accompanied Amy out of the woods and back onto the grassy slope. He looked up at the islands floating in the sky and wondered which of them was Numblebrook Island Prison. Amy took a long yellow whistle from her pocket and blew into it. To Ben's astonishment, within seconds a bright green dragon was flying towards them with huge spiked wings. It circled in the air several times, before gliding down and landing a few feet away from them on the grass. Ben stumbled backwards in surprise.

"Don't worry," laughed the girl, "this is Shami, she's my pet dragon and she's very friendly."

Shami knelt down and Amy patted her gently. Shami licked her hand fondly and blinked her huge, friendly eyes. Amy then held on to one of the dragon's spikes and swung her right leg over her back. "Hurry up, jump on!" she shouted to Ben. "It will be going dark soon. If we hurry we can just about make it to the Citadel before nightfall."

Ben was alarmed and really not too keen on the idea of climbing onto a strange dragon's back. Other options raced through his mind. If he stayed here he might risk being caught by King Ados' guards and locked away in Numblebrook Island Prison. He gazed at Amy and the dragon in silence. He was too afraid to stay here alone and Amy seemed like the safest option. With his mind made up, he tiptoed quietly over to Shami and cautiously placed his hand on the dragon's side, wondering how on earth he would manage to climb onto such a large beast. The dragon's scales felt rough to touch, and he could feel the movement of the gigantic animal's breathing beneath his fingers.

"Here, let me help you up," shouted Amy, as she reached out her hand. Ben gripped it tightly and she helped haul him up onto Shami's large, spiked back. "Put your arms around my waist and hold on tight!" she shouted excitedly.

Before Ben could protest, the dragon spread her enormous wings and rose up into the sky.

Chapter 3

The Citadel

Ben could feel himself rising higher and higher, and was too afraid to open his eyes. The air felt cool and the breeze was fresh on his windswept face.

"Look at the view, Benjamin Giddle; it's beautiful from up here," shouted Amy. She was sitting just in front of Ben, but still had to shout to make herself heard over the sound of the wind.

Ben slowly opened his eyes and, despite his fear of heights, gasped in awe at the breathtaking view. They were high up in the blue sky, above the floating islands and far above the land. He looked down at the islands and noticed several dragons in many bright colours gliding through the sky.

"Do the dragons live on the islands?" he shouted nervously.

"Yes," replied Amy, "most of them, anyway. Some of them, like Shami, have owners, but they usually go back to the islands at nightfall."

"Are they all friendly?"

"Not the red dragons, they are vicious and live alone. Never approach a red dragon, or you could pay for it with your life!"

As Shami began to change direction, Ben held on tightly and leaned to the side to keep his balance. Amy pointed towards the hillside below, and Ben saw what appeared to be a fairy-tale white castle surrounded by a wide moat. A huge bridge crossed the water and led to the gigantic, wooden front gates. Guards appeared almost like dots, positioned high on the castle walls between the four pointed turrets.

"That's King Ados' palace; it's called Cottisham Castle. It's a beautiful place, but nobody dares to go there as King Ados doesn't allow visitors. It used to belong to the Moonbeamers when they ruled the land."

Ben stared in wonder at the magnificent, majestic palace, until something suddenly caught his eye far above the castle. "What's that?" he asked, pointing to one of the floating islands which was bigger than the others. Two large buildings stood on the island, and Ben was horrified to see people in chains.

"That's Numblebrook Island Prison," replied Amy. "That's where the King sends anyone who dares to disobey his rules. The Unicerons are his guards, and prisoners are locked in cells at night. During the day they have to do manual work, whatever the King requests. Nobody can escape because of where they are, and most people who get sent to the prison are never seen again."

Ben shuddered at the thought. "What a ghastly place! How do they get up there?"

"The King had a special prison chariot made. He owns a huge red dragon which is under his spell. He uses the dragon to pull the chariot and take prisoners to and from the island."

A chill went through Ben, and he prayed he would never have to visit such a vile place.

They carried on flying for what seemed like hours. They passed over rocky mountains, deep ravines, dense forests and bright blue lakes. Ben's fear of heights gradually subsided and he began to feel at ease and started to enjoy the journey.

By the time Shami started to glide downwards, it was beginning to go dark.

"Look, Ben, we're nearly there... that's the Citadel," shouted Amy, pointing to what looked like a small city built into the side of a mountain. Balconies bowed out and waterfalls cascaded down between stone buildings and luscious green trees. Some of the large balconies contained gardens full of brightly coloured flowers and shrubs. They landed gently on the ground at the base of the mountain outside some huge metal gates, and quickly jumped down from

Shami's back. Despite the fact that Ben had begun to relax during the flight, he felt relieved to feel the ground beneath his feet again.

"Good girl, Shami," said Amy. She took something from her pocket, and the dragon took it eagerly. "Ginger apples," she said. "It's her favourite treat."

Amy was obviously very fond of the dragon, and she stroked her head lovingly as she ate. She then turned to walk towards the gates, where a pleasant-looking Moonbeamer with elfin features sat in a tall sentry box.

Ben looked in surprise at the slight haze around him, which shimmered as he moved and spoke.

"What can I do for you?" asked the Moonbeamer politely.

"We would like to speak to the senior Moonbeamers if possible," replied Amy.

"They have an important meeting tonight and have asked not to be disturbed!"

"Is there any chance they could just spare us a few minutes? We really need a little advice. Please, it's very important!" pleaded Amy.

"As I've already told you, they have an important meeting tonight and they have asked not to be disturbed; not unless it's urgent."

"But this *is* urgent!" stressed Amy. "My friend Benjamin needs to find his way back to Labyrinth Junction and we have no idea how to find it."

"Labyrinth Junction hasn't been seen for years. The Moonbeamers won't be able to help you."

"But I've just come from there earlier today!" proclaimed Ben. "One minute it was there and the next minute it had vanished. My mum will be wondering where I am!"

"That can't possibly be true… telling fibs won't help you!" the Moonbeamer snapped, becoming a little impatient.

"Honestly, I'm telling the truth – why don't you believe me?" begged Ben as he felt all hope starting to fade.

At first the Moonbeamer looked unconvinced, but then he slowly started to study Ben with interest. "Well, you certainly don't look very much like the children from around here. You haven't got yellow hair, for a start!"

"He's a Giddle!" exclaimed Amy excitedly. "Can't you tell?"

"Well, I've never seen a Giddle before! If that's the case, you had better come in!"

Ben's eyes brightened as the Moonbeamer climbed down from the sentry box and banged on the metal gates.

"Open up, open up!" he shouted.

The screeching of bolts being drawn back could be heard, before the huge gates creaked open. The sentry signalled to another Moonbeamer in red clothing and whispered something in his ear. The Moonbeamer studied Ben curiously before gliding off through the large doorway at the base of the mountain, shimmering as he went.

"He's a messenger," said the sentry. "He's advising the senior Moonbeamers of your arrival."

He then turned and called to a pretty female Moonbeamer. "Tia, I need you to escort these two children to the Great Hall; they wish to speak to the senior Moonbeamers."

"Follow me," replied Tia with a kind, sympathetic smile as she began to glide in the direction of the large building.

Ben and Amy followed her up the path towards the main entrance. Ben was astounded at just how tall the Moonbeamers were. They looked similar to elves, although he had always read in storybooks that elves were very tiny. But the Moonbeamers were tall, much taller than he was, and they didn't walk, they glided a few inches above the floor in a strange, shimmering light. Tia had long raven hair, and her sparkling, tawny eyes twinkled with kindness. Her flawless ivory skin shone with beauty, and Ben thought she was probably the most beautiful being he had ever seen. She led them through the doorway and along a wide hallway. The walls were lined with wooden panels, each displaying a wonderful carving.

They reached what Ben imagined was the biggest and most majestic staircase he had ever seen, and he looked up in awe as they started to climb. Eventually they reached the top and huge, double arched doors towered ahead of them. Tia stopped outside and knocked gently. The doors immediately began to open inwards, and a Moonbeamer in red clothing beckoned them in. Tia led Ben and Amy through the doors into an enormous hall. Ben looked around in amazement. The high ceiling was covered in archaic paintings, and it reminded him of pictures of the Sistine Chapel he had studied in books. The windows were large and arch-shaped, and majestic pillars stood around the room. In the centre a group of Moonbeamers were seated around an enormous stone table. One of them stood as they entered.

"Welcome to the Citadel. My name's Hal," he exclaimed as he held out his hand, his eyes shimmering with warmth.

Like the other Moonbeamers, he was tall and slender with long dark hair and bright chestnut-brown eyes. Ben thought he was a handsome man with a warm smile, and immediately felt at ease.

"I understand that you entered our land through Labyrinth Junction earlier today and would like our help to locate it again?" Hal asked Ben directly.

"Yes, that's right," stammered Ben, hope swelling in his stomach.

"Tell me what happened?" asked Hal inquisitively.

Ben told the Moonbeamers how he had come to find Labyrinth Junction, about the old lady who resembled a witch and the red sweets she had given him. He told them about the passageways and his arrival into their land. He also told them about his encounter with King Ados, and how he had become invisible when he ate one of the sweets. Amy helped fill in some of the details, and the Moonbeamers listened intently without interruption. When Ben had finished, the Moonbeamers were quiet. They asked for drinks and food to be brought for their guests, and Ben and Amy accepted them gladly. So much had happened that day that Ben had completely forgotten that he hadn't eaten since breakfast – apart from the invisibility sweet of course! As he and Amy ate, the Moonbeamers watched and whispered amongst themselves before approaching their guests.

"I understand your worry and your need to get back to your family. Your friend Amy was right to bring you here. If I could help you, I truly would, but the truth is, we are no longer able to locate the Junction ourselves. The trouble is, King Ados' father took away most of our magical powers when he stole the kingdom from us. The magic that remains, we are forbidden to use. If we wield the old magic to try to locate the passageway, the King will know immediately. If he discovers that the Moonbeamers are using magic again, most of us will be slain and the rest will be taken to Numblebrook Island Prison. Unfortunately, that is not a risk we can take and our priority must remain with our fellow Moonbeamers. I am truly sorry… I wish we could help you return home, Benjamin, but unfortunately we cannot."

Ben's hopes disintegrated, and Amy regarded him sympathetically.

"What am I to do, then?" he pleaded.

"You are welcome to stay here with us," replied Hal. "You are a Giddle, and you are therefore not safe in this land. If King Ados finds you, he will imprison you at the very least. If you stay here in the Citadel, we will keep you safe. We hope one day to overpower the King and return the realm to the Moonbeamers. If this ever happens, we will again have the use of our magic and I will gladly locate the Junction for you myself. But until that day comes, my hands are tied. My priority has to be the safety of the other Moonbeamers… I am sorry."

"How do you hope to overpower the King?" Ben asked, trying to cling on to any last bit of hope.

"Firstly we have to discover how to reach the Enchanter's Orb," replied Hal. "The King obtains his power from the Orb, which he has hidden away in a secret location. The Orb serves only its master, but that master can change if someone finds the Orb and chants the magic spell. The Orb also has a hold over the Unicerons and supplies the power to the Sword of Gwyntog. Both will only serve their master, and unfortunately, at this time their master is King Ados. But we hope to find the Orb and change this!"

"Do you know how to find the Enchanter's Orb?" asked Ben.

"Unfortunately not; we have been trying to locate it for many years. King Ados' father hid it well, and the only people who know its location are King Ados and his heirs."

Silence followed. Ben liked the Moonbeamers and was sure that they would protect him, but he wanted to go home. He wanted to see his parents, his brothers and sisters, and his dog. He had fought with his brothers and his sisters had irritated him, but now he just wanted to see their faces again, and his heart wrenched in sadness.

As he looked towards Hal, he noticed a large book on the stone table in front of him. On the cover of the book were the words *Haligan Lexin*. Something about the name seemed familiar, and Ben started to rack his brains as to why this was. "What's your name?" he spluttered, intrigued.

"Why, Hal, of course!"

"No, your full name?" asked Ben hastily.

"My full name is Haligan Lexin. Why?" he answered curiously.

All of a sudden Ben remembered why the name sounded so familiar. He quickly searched his pockets and pulled out the green envelope the old witch had given to him. In big letters across the front it said, *PRIVATE & CONFIDENTIAL*, and underneath, *For the attention of HALIGAN LEXIN*.

"I had completely forgotten! The old lady asked me to deliver this to you. She wanted me to pay her ten noggings for passage through Labyrinth Junction, but I didn't have any noggings… I didn't even know what noggings were! So she told me that I could only pass through if I delivered this letter to someone called Haligan Lexin. She wouldn't tell me who that was. She said I had to find out for myself!"

Ben eagerly handed the envelope to Hal, who looked at it suspiciously. He slowly opened the envelope and pulled out a green sheet of paper. His eyes looked down at the words it contained, and he remained silent for what seemed like a long time.

When he eventually looked up, a smile appeared on his face and he slowly began to read:

Down in the keep
Lies the Enchanter's Orb.
The magic that it oozes
Is used to fuel the Sword.

It is a perilous journey
Down to this magic globe,
But those who seek to rule us
Must crack the number code.

This Enchanter's Orb
Will serve but one man well:
The last to hold the Orb
And chant the magic spell.

Deep in the eucalyptus wood
Lies the Gothic Well.
How many steps
To ring the golden bell?

Hidden in the caves
Is the red dragon's lair.
Count the spikes on his back;
Beware of the bear.

Down in the glen
Dwells the wise old man.
How can he hear you?
LISTEN to his wisdom if you can.

Deep in the sea
Rest the Ancient Scrolls.
Be sure to read them carefully;
Beware the deadly souls.

The riddle reveals the spell,
But the numbers are all mixed up high.
Only one chance to get them right;
They are all 'pie in the sky'.

After Hal had finished reading the contents of the letter, the room remained silent. But slowly, smiles started to appear on the Moonbeamers' faces. Then came joyous laughter, and Hal turned to Ben.

"Well, Ben, for two decades we have hunted for clues to help us find the missing Orb. It appears that you have just provided us with these. This is a riddle – a riddle that can help us find the Enchanter's Orb and maybe restore the crown to the Moonbeamers. Benjamin Giddle, I think you have been sent here for a reason: to help us find the Orb and restore peace and happiness here in Numblebrook." The Moonbeamer stood and raised his glass. "Here's to finding the Enchanter's Orb!" he declared.

"To finding the Enchanter's Orb!" The other senior Moonbeamers joyfully joined the toast.

Hal then turned to Ben and raised his glass again. "And here's to Benjamin Giddle!"

"To Benjamin Giddle!" everyone cheered in delight.

Chapter 4
The Riddle

Ben and Amy were given a room at the Citadel that night, and they talked well into the early hours. Amy explained that she was an only child and had become an orphan at the age of six. Her parents had owned a small farm in a village near to the palace. They had possessed a handful of sheep, cows and chickens, and had grown all their own vegetables. Her father would travel to nearby towns selling wool, eggs, milk and other produce. He worked extremely hard to bring in the money, and they were comfortable. Life was happy and peaceful for them, until King Ados passed a new law prohibiting farmers from selling their own goods. This law stated that all farm produce was to be sold via a large Sunday market that was run by the state. The supplies sold at this market were to be heavily taxed, the tax monies going directly to the King.

This new law was leaving farmers virtually penniless and struggling to survive. Most sold to passers-by, family and friends, but the King forbade this. He discovered that farmers from Amy's village had been selling their stock illegally; something they needed to do to earn a sufficient income. One dark night the King ordered his guards to burn the village and its farms to the ground, as a warning to any other farmer who dared to sell crops and produce without paying the hefty taxes. Sadly, Amy's parents died in the fire. Amy escaped by jumping from her bedroom window and running into the nearby woods.

The survivors rebuilt their houses and tried to resurrect their businesses. They cared for Amy and gave her a home, but it wasn't the same as having her family, and nobody noticed if she was gone for days on end.

She stumbled upon Shami one warm summer's day whilst exploring in the woods. Shami had been hurt in a trap, and Amy bandaged her wounds and nursed her back to health. Whenever Amy whistled, the dragon would be there within minutes, and Amy felt that Shami was her only true family now.

Ben thought this was a very sad story, and could not imagine what it must be like to be an orphan. Amy hated King Ados for killing her parents and she, more than anyone, wanted the crown restored to the Moonbeamers.

The next morning Ben woke before Amy. The room had an enormous, square window that overlooked the city, and he sat for a long time, watching the Moonbeamers' daily activities. He heard a gentle tap at the door and Tia stood outside, holding a large tray of food and drink.

"Good morning, Benjamin, I've brought you both some breakfast; I thought you might be hungry. Did you sleep well?"

"Yes, I did, thank you. Thanks for the breakfast; I'm starving! I had better wake Amy."

"Hal has arranged a meeting at ten o'clock in the Great Hall. I will collect you and Amy just before. Enjoy your breakfast."

Just after ten o'clock, they entered the Great Hall. Amy's freshly washed hair shone in the morning sunlight, and Ben thought she appeared to have regained a liveliness in her step after the painful memories of the previous night.

"Good morning. Did you sleep well?" asked Hal with a smile.

Ben and Amy both nodded.

"We have a lot to discuss this morning… we have a riddle to solve! Would you both like to join our council and help us to solve this rhyme?"

"Oh, yes please!" Amy chirped in delight.

She seemed really eager, and Ben noticed how happy she appeared. He thought that she probably

relished the idea of staying with the Moonbeamers, as she had no family of her own and the Moonbeamers were really kind and welcoming people. They smiled at her response and turned to look at Ben.

"Me too!" he replied enthusiastically, knowing that solving the riddle and finding the Enchanter's Orb was his only hope of locating Labyrinth Junction.

"Excellent!" said Hal, smiling.

A short and stocky Moonbeamer introduced himself as Josiah. He wasn't willowy and lithe like the others; he had chiselled features and broad, strong shoulders. He unfolded a large piece of paper on which he had copied the riddle, and laid it on the table for everyone to see.

"Does anyone have any ideas?" asked Hal.

"Let's have a look at the first few verses," Josiah suggested.

Everyone agreed that this was a good starting point, and Hal began to read:

Down in the keep
Lies the Enchanter's Orb.
The magic that it oozes
Is used to fuel the Sword.

It is a perilous journey
Down to this magic globe,
But those who seek to rule us
Must crack the number code.

This Enchanter's Orb
Will serve but one man well:
The last to hold the Orb
And chant the magic spell.

"We are already aware of how the Orb functions; it serves only one living soul and it supplies the power to the Sword of Gwyntog," said Hal. "The poem implies that the Orb is in the keep. When my father was king, I spent much of my childhood at Cottisham Castle. It was common knowledge that there existed a keep beneath the castle, but I was not allowed to explore it. I was told that it was a dark and dangerous place, so it makes sense that the Orb is hidden there within King Ados' reach."

"It also mentions a number code!" exclaimed Josiah. "Maybe this suggests that the Orb is locked away and a code is needed to free it?"

"And it mentions a magic spell!" declared Ben excitedly. "Do you know what the spell is?"

"Unfortunately not, Ben!" replied Hal with a sigh. "But I'm hoping that the riddle will lead us to it!"

"Let's read on," suggested Ballin, a softly spoken Moonbeamer, whose white teeth flashed brightly against his tanned jolly face. "I'm hoping that the rest of the rhyme will give us a clue as to where to start looking!"

Smiles crept over the group's faces as Hal read on:

Deep in the eucalyptus wood
Lies the Gothic Well.
How many steps
To ring the golden bell?

"This must be the first clue to help solve the number code!" said Josiah eagerly. "There are many eucalyptus woods in our land, but I have never heard of one which contains a gothic well!"

"I think I may know of this well!" Amy uttered in excitement.

The Moonbeamers looked at her intently, eager to hear what she had to say.

"One day Shami and I had travelled quite far and we stopped for a rest in a eucalyptus wood. I was exploring, and out of the corner of my eye, I noticed an old well. It looked as if it hadn't been tended to or used in many years. The stones were crumbling and the overgrowth almost hid it from view. I cannot recall any steps, though I could have missed them. To be honest, it looked rather spooky and I was happy to keep a safe distance away."

"Would you be able to find your way back to this well?" asked Hal hopefully.

"I was a long way from home, but I'm sure Shami would help. She has a very good memory and knows these lands well."

"It would be of great benefit to us if Shami could remember the way," replied Hal. "It's a good starting point, and we can always widen our search if it turns out that this is not the well we seek."

Amy smiled with renewed importance after giving the Moonbeamers such vital information.

Hal slowly read out the next verse:

Hidden in the caves
Is the red dragon's lair.
Count the spikes on his back;
Beware of the bear.

"Red dragons are ferocious. It would take a brave being to enter one's lair and count the spikes on its back!" declared Ballin.

"Maybe I could eat one of my red sweets and become invisible?" suggested Ben.

"That's very courageous of you, Ben!" added Hal. "But first, we need to locate this lair: red dragons live in many corners of this land."

"The answer might be found in the ancient manuscripts," added Ballin. "Red dragons live for thousands of years, so if one particular lair is important it may have been documented at some point."

"I will arrange for the librarians to search through the manuscripts for any information. If none can be found, we will speak with the village folk," said Hal. "The last line of the verse states *Beware of the bear*. This I do not understand, as bears have been extinct in this land for thousands of years. Maybe this is a clue as to where the cave is. Again, I will ask the librarians to look for any information about bears. Any other suggestions?"

The room remained quiet, so Hal moved on:

Down in the glen
Dwells the wise old man.
How can he hear you?
LISTEN to his wisdom if you can.

"There are many glens and I don't know of any wise old man. Again, this is something we could ask the villagers about; if there is a man of great wisdom residing close by, they will no doubt know of him."

"It doesn't mention finding a number in this verse!" added Amy curiously.

"Perhaps it will become clearer when we find the wise man," suggested Hal, before reading the next verse:

Deep in the sea
Rest the Ancient Scrolls.
Be sure to read them carefully;
Beware the deadly souls.

"In history books, I have read that there was once an ancient city called Xallanpolis," Hal advised. "It is rumoured that Xallanpolis was swept away in the floods. Our ancestors believed that the city is now under the sea, but as it has never been found, and many now believe that this is just an old wives' tale. Divers spent many years searching for Xallanpolis, but no evidence of an ancient city was ever recovered."

"Maybe the wise old man can tell us more about this?" suggested a chirpy-looking Moonbeamer, with a round face and jolly sparkling eyes named Shadrack.

"Maybe," replied Hal. "Again, it never mentions a number. Perhaps the number is written in the Ancient Scrolls. I will ask the librarians to check the old books for any information about this ancient city and its scrolls." He wrote something down on a piece of paper before reciting the final verse:

The riddle reveals the spell,
But the numbers are all mixed up high.
Only one chance to get them right;
They are all 'pie in the sky'.

"Maybe this implies that once we have discovered the numbers, we must rearrange them into a specific order," added Ballin. "*Only one chance to get them right*. Perhaps something awful will occur if they are not arranged correctly!"

"Maybe," replied Josiah, very apprehensively. "What do you think *pie in the sky* means?"

"It can mean a promise of something good that is unlikely to happen. It probably has a double meaning here, in that the numbers are jumbled up, and also that this mission is a hard one to achieve," Hal answered.

"It has another meaning too," added Ben softly.

The rest of the group looked at him intently.

"I learnt about it at school. We were studying old sayings and their meanings. It also means 'a reward that comes after death'!"

The room was silent. Everyone had the same thought: if this was true, then whose death was the riddle referring to? Fear quickly spread throughout the room.

Chapter 5
The Gothic Well

The next few days were spent at the Citadel making preparations for the forthcoming journey. There was some excitement about the mission, but they were also apprehensive about what dangers might lie ahead. It was decided that Hal, Josiah, Ballin, Shadrack, Amy and Ben would go in search of the Gothic Well. The rest of the Moonbeamers would stay at the Citadel and continue to search through the ancient books for any information that might help them to solve the riddle. The search party would take Shami and two other dragons by the names of Kamar and Sissy, fly to an old monument mid-way and rest there before commencing their journey.

The evening before they were due to leave, the six members of the party met for a final time in the Great

Hall. Hal handed each of them large, sandy-coloured pebbles.

"I want you each to take one of these. They are called moonstones, and were used by the Moonbeamers in ancient times for communication."

"How?" Ben asked.

"If you rub the stone between your hands to make it warm and then utter a person's name, that person's stone will begin to glow. If that person then looks into their stone, they will see an image of you and you will be able to communicate. For hundreds of years we Moonbeamers used these as a means of communication, but they do use a small amount of magic. King Ados has forbidden us to use magic, and if we do so we will be punished harshly. Because of this, we have not used the moonstones since the Orb was stolen from us. However, as the stones only use a very small amount of magic, hopefully the King's spies won't notice. But we do need to be cautious, and therefore the stones must only be used in an emergency."

"Can we experiment with them now?" asked Ben excitedly.

Hal narrowed his eyes. "No! As I've said, they can only be used in emergencies. You must look after the stones carefully and keep them safe!"

Disappointed, Ben reluctantly slipped his stone into his pocket.

The next morning they were given supplies for their journey and Tia wished them luck. Although Ben and Amy were excited, they also felt sad to be leaving the safety and warmth of the Citadel. The Moonbeamers had been welcoming and they had both felt a sense of belonging there.

Shadrack announced it was time to go, and they climbed aboard the dragons, travelling in pairs. Ben flew with Hal on Kamar and Hal told him tales of times gone by and how King Ados had come to rule. He told him how the King's father, King Xen, had tricked the Moonbeamers and stolen the Enchanter's Orb, keeping it for himself. The Unicerons had turned their backs on the Moonbeamers and sworn allegiance to King Xen. Hal did not think the Unicerons enjoyed serving King Xen, as he was a mean and evil king, but the Orb's magic controlled and enchanted them. King Xen had ruled the land for fifteen years until his death five years ago. On his death, his son Ados was crowned and given the Enchanter's Orb and the Sword of Gwyntog. King Ados was even crueller than his father, and nobody in the land favoured this new king.

Ben told Hal about his family, about his parents and siblings and his dog. He wondered what they were doing and felt sad that he had not seen them for several days. They would be extremely fretful and upset about his disappearance, and this worried Ben greatly. Hal tried to reassure him and promised he would do everything he could to help Ben return home. Ben was grateful for this, for he knew that the Moonbeamers were good people and hoped that they would once again rule this beautiful land.

Halfway through their journey, they rested by a huge monument, and Ben admired the scenery surrounding them. A long, narrow valley stretched out before him and the luscious green fields spanned for miles around. The monument was in the shape of a tall, slender man wearing a crown of flowers; he held a staff in his hand and children were seated at his feet. The inscription at the bottom read, *In memory of King Semba, who served this land well.*

"Who was King Semba?" Ben asked.

"He was my great-great-great-grandfather," Hal said. "He was a very popular king, and the whole land mourned when he died. He was a great inspiration to the Moonbeamers."

The six members of the group sat and gathered their thoughts, resting before they continued on their journey. Shami grazed alongside the other two dragons, Kamar and Sissy. They were green like Shami, but taller and not as gentle-looking.

"Amy, why don't you and Ben ride on Shami and guide the way? Hopefully Shami will remember the route," said Hal. "Ballin, you can fly with me on Kamar. Josiah and Shadrack, you both go with Sissy. How long do you think it will take for us to reach the well, Amy?"

"I'm not sure. It's hard to remember exactly how far it was, but I know we made quite a long journey that day. I would say it's at least a two-hour flight."

"Then we must waste no more time and get on our way immediately. By the look of those clouds in the distance, a storm could be heading this way."

Shami led the way and they travelled at speed. They flew over tall mountains, deep valleys and green forests. They spotted villages dotted around and farmers tending their crops. Ben saw the coastline in the distance, with the sea stretching away far into the horizon. He spotted an island with what looked like a tiny church and a very small harbour. There were a couple of boats moored up, but he couldn't see any people or any houses. They flew past beautiful golden, sandy beaches and steep white cliffs which ran down to the shoreline. The air was warm and fresh, and Ben enjoyed the feel of the wind on his face.

Eventually, they turned back inland and began to descend, heading towards a clearing in the middle of a thick forest. Once they were safe on the ground, Amy looked around, trying to gather her bearings. She noticed what looked like a pathway into the wood and signalled for the others to follow. The dragons stayed in the clearing, grazing on the rich green grass, whilst Ben and the Moonbeamers followed Amy into the forest. Ben looked up at the eucalyptus trees and hoped that their presence was a promising sign. The wood was very dense and thick, but luckily the sun still managed to shine through the tall trees.

Eventually they came to what looked like a huge cluster of bushes, and Ben was intrigued when Amy went over to them and began peering through the leaves and branches.

"It's here, I've found it!" she screeched in excitement.

They started ripping away the branches and, to their delight, inside the overgrowth they found a circular stone wall. It was built from a very old, thick grey stone and was beginning to crumble in places. The circle of stones was about fifteen feet in diameter, and Ben thought he had never seen a well of such enormous size. The six friends cleared a path to the wall and approached it to peer over the edge. They were unable to see the bottom of the well; it looked like a dark pit which went on forever. Hal picked up a stone and dropped it into the abyss. They listened to see if they could hear it hit the bottom, but no sound emerged from within, and Ben imagined it must be a very long way down. Ballin shone his lantern into the well, and they noticed steps that spiralled downwards against the walls. In the middle was a steep drop. There were no railings and the steps looked old, crumbling and extremely dangerous.

"What do you think?" asked Josiah apprehensively.

"It certainly looks like the well described in the riddle. This wood contains lots of eucalyptus trees and this well is definitely very old," replied Hal. "The only way to find out for certain is to go down and have a look."

"I'll go!" said Ben hastily. "Those steps look very narrow and I'm much smaller than you Moonbeamers. I'm less likely to fall!"

"I'll accompany you; you can't go down there alone," replied Hal. "Three of us should go down and three stay up here and act as lookouts. What about you, Ballin – will you join us?"

"Yes, I would be happy to," replied Ballin, not looking very convinced.

"We each need to count the steps," announced Hal. "The riddle asks how many steps there are to ring the golden bell, and it looks like quite a long way down. If we all count the steps, there is less chance of an error being made."

Ben and Ballin agreed and quickly climbed over the wall to where the steps began. Hal went first, with Ben following and Ballin at the rear. Ben tied a lantern to his chest, freeing his hands to give himself as much balance as possible. The bright lamp and the shimmering lights produced by the Moonbeamers lit up the well, and they began their descent. The steps were old and worn and Ben noticed that they were damp, cracked and crumbling in places. He chose not to dwell on this too much and carried on descending, carefully counting each step as he went. He used the wall to guide himself, and it felt cold and wet beneath his fingertips.

Suddenly, out of the corner of his eye, Ben thought he saw something move and stopped in fear. A chill went through him as he pointed to the far side of the well. The others followed his gaze and to their astonishment saw what appeared to be a pair of eyes in the stone wall. Hal felt a sense of trepidation as he moved his lamp to the right and to his horror saw hundreds of pairs which shone angrily from within the walls. Ben's blood ran cold as he quickly moved a few inches away from the stone side, held up his lamp and soon realised that there were eyes everywhere, even just inches from him. He had an incredible urge to step away from them, but knew that if he did so, he would lose his balance and fall to the bottom of the well.

"What are they?" he blurted, horrified.

"I think someone must have cast a spell on the well to make these eyes appear," replied Hal nervously, trying to hide his fear. "They are probably here just to frighten us away. I think we have found the Gothic Well, and someone or something does not want us here. We have already descended nearly one hundred steps and I'm sure we must have passed many of these eyes. If they could harm us in any way, they would have done so by now. I think we are nearing the bottom of the well. We should continue going down!"

He turned and carried on descending. In all the confusion, Ben had almost forgotten how many steps he had counted, but thankfully his memory did not let him down. So far he had been feeling his way along the wall of the well whilst counting the steps. This had helped him to balance, but now that he had seen the eyes, he was too afraid to touch the rock. Worry snaked through him as he continued down.

After descending a few more metres, Hal shouted up that he had reached the bottom, and Ben felt an overwhelming sense of relief and quickly joined him.

"How many steps did you count?" asked Hal, eager to escape the strange well.

"I counted 162," stuttered Ballin.

"Me too!" said Ben anxiously.

"Excellent," replied Hal. "That's the same as I counted, so we can be pretty certain that we haven't made a mistake. The riddle says, *How many steps to ring the golden bell?* Let's look around to see if we can find this bell."

They held out their lanterns, searching in the darkness.

"Over here!" shouted Ben, trying to sound hopeful through the anxiety that swirled around him.

The others walked over to where he was standing. A little alcove was set in one of the walls and within it was what appeared to be a small well, a miniature version of the one they had just descended. It looked identical, except that this well had a bell above it, hanging from the stony ceiling of the alcove. The bell was golden in colour and had a small, thin cord hanging from it.

"Do you think we are meant to ring it?" asked

Ben quietly. It struck him as odd that they were whispering when there was nobody else around, but he felt uneasy in the darkness.

"I think we should," replied Ballin. "The riddle asked how many steps there are to *ring* the bell. We have climbed a long way down and I certainly don't want to have to come back here because we missed something."

"Me too," answered Ben, shuddering at the thought.

"Very well, stand back just in case something happens, though I'm sure everything will be fine," Hal advised.

Ben and Ballin took a few steps backwards and Hal reached out to take the end of the cord. He slowly drew his hand to the side and released the rope. It swung back, and the bell let out a loud and piercing chime. They hadn't expected it to ring so loudly, and immediately covered their ears with their hands. The bell chimed once and the cord slowly stopped swinging. Then they heard a different sound coming from within the small well. It was a grating sound, like rocks being dragged along a stone floor. They approached and looked downwards. To their surprise, what they thought was the bottom of the well was moving to one side and an opening began to appear. The three of them watched until the stone panel came to a standstill and Hal peered inside to see what was beneath. They found themselves looking at an axe, and a shiny glass box bearing a lock. The box was quite large, and placed on top was an old, rusty-looking key.

Hal cautiously lifted the box from the well, not certain whether this could be some kind of trick. He slotted the key into the lock and it fitted perfectly. Slowly, the lid was lifted to reveal a small box-shaped jewellery case made of red velvet. They looked at each other dubiously. Hal bent down to retrieve it from the well, and as he opened it, the others eagerly looked over his shoulder to see what was inside. Wrapped in a soft, white piece of cloth was a round turquoise coin. On one side was a picture of a bear, and on the reverse was a dragon's head. The coin was smooth and appeared to be made out of some kind of gemstone. Its discovery posed many questions: why was it here, and what was its purpose? They looked at each other in confusion, before deciding not to dwell on the matter until they had escaped from the strange and sinister eyes. Hal put the small box inside an inner pocket of his cape and then bent down to reach the axe. It was about a foot in length, with a wooden handle and a silver-tipped blade.

"What do you think the axe is for?" whispered Ben.

"I have no idea, but I think it would be a good idea to take it with us," advised Hal.

He picked up the axe and they quickly turned to leave. There was tension in the air and they felt uneasy. They ran back to the steps and started their ascent, trying to ignore the perculiar eyes in the walls which watched them with intent. All of a sudden, to Ben's horror, he felt something grabbing at his legs and he let out a roaring scream. Hal looked in Ben's direction, and with dread saw that beneath the scornful blinking eyes, a nose and mouth had appeared, and arms were protruding from the walls. The hands had long fingers with razor-sharp claws. The mouths were muttering uncontrollably, and hissing sounds could be heard

loudly. Ben tried frantically to shake his leg free as claws ripped through his trouser leg and into his flesh. Immediately realising what the axe was for, Hal turned to Ben and struck out at the moving arms. As the blade bit into them, the accompanying face in the wall seemed to howl in pain and the hands disappeared back into the stone. Ben's blood ran cold as he clambered as fast as he could up the steps, in such a panic that he could no longer feel the pain in his leg. More arms appeared, and Hal hacked at them as they tried to hurry up the steps. They had to climb close to the edge, as far away from the stone wall as possible, but underfoot was very slippery and if they lost their footing they would topple and fall to the bottom of the well. Ballin had taken out his sword and he too was swinging at the arms, trying to stop the hands from grabbing at their clothing and legs. More and more faces were appearing the higher they climbed, and brave Hal battled to keep the arms at bay. The more he hacked, the louder the wailing sounds became, and the noise was piercing. Ben felt a sense of helplessness and bit back a scream.

Luckily, Amy and the others had heard the shrieks from the top of the well and instantly a rope appeared.

"Quick, grab the rope and we will haul you up!" shouted Shadrack.

"Grasp the rope quickly, Ben. You are the only one without a weapon!" yelled Hal, trying to make himself heard above the loud wails.

Ben grabbed the rope and shouted up that he was ready. The others quickly hauled him to the top of the well and then sent the rope back down for Hal and Ballin. Ballin was the next to take the rope, and Hal stayed on the steps, trying to stop the evil from within the walls from attacking. He was unable to climb any further, and tried to swing the axe at the claws, but they were too overpowering. They had a tight hold of his cloak, and he could feel the pain in his chest where they were gashing at his skin. He dropped the axe whilst trying to grab hold of the rope, and it crashed to the bottom of the well. Fear twisted through his gut as the others tried hard to haul him up, but the claws gripped him tightly and he was unable to break free. As he frantically kicked at the hands, he could feel his clothes tear as they slowly began to lose their grip.

Suddenly, he swung free and felt himself being hauled upwards. Hope fluttered inside him as he was hauled higher and he realised he was free from the eerie well and its evil claws. Splashes of rain hit him as Josiah and Shadrack pulled him over the stone wall and laid him on the ground to bind his wounds. Amy had already wrapped several bandages around Ben's arms and legs, and Hal could see that Ballin was also injured. Although Ben was hurt, exultation surged through him as he realised how lucky he was to be alive.

"You've been a long time down there," exclaimed Shadrack. "We were getting worried. The storm is fast approaching. We need to find the dragons and get out of here quickly. Are you all well enough to walk to the clearing?"

They all nodded, and Amy was sent ahead to whistle for the dragons. The skies were dark and the wind was howling. Rain lashed down as they tried to escape the horrors of the wood. Hal clung tightly to Josiah for support as they made their way to the clearing. The others followed and they hurried as quickly as they could, eager to be free from the storm.

When they arrived at the clearing, Amy was tending to the dragons and Shami, in particular, looked edgy. Amy tried to calm her as they climbed onto the dragons' backs.

"If we lose each other, meet back at the Citadel," shouted Shadrack. "Hopefully, the Unicerons won't be on the lookout in this storm."

Sissy, the dragon Shadrack and Hal were riding, rose up into the air, and Kamar quickly followed with Ballin and Josiah clinging on tightly. Shami still seemed uneasy, and Amy gave her a gentle kick as they too rose into the air. The storm was becoming ferocious and rain lashed their faces. Ben thought it felt like needles against his flesh, and half-shut his eyes to ease the pain. The wind was roaring and the heavy grey clouds travelled rapidly through the sky towards them. All of a sudden, there was a huge flash of lightning followed by a tremendous boom of thunder. Shami jerked in fear as she flew downwards, closer to the trees.

"Up, Shami, up! We need to get away from the trees. Fly higher, Shami!" Amy cried in terror, trying to make herself heard through the loud, violent storm.

Shami was afraid and reluctant to fly closer to the thunder and lightning. Without warning, a huge flash of forked lightning struck out across the sky. Shami made a sudden dive, heading for the forest floor, dodging between the trees and catching branches as she fell. That's when Ben spotted them: Unicerons in the wood, hundreds of them, weaving their way between the trees! Maybe they had been out hunting and got caught up in the storm? Or perhaps the bell in the well and the mysterious faces and hands in the stone had somehow alerted them? Ben pointed to them as Amy tried to steer Shami away before they were spotted. But it was too late – the Unicerons had seen them!

They began shouting and pointing towards the dragon. Amy cried out to Shami and kicked her sides, trying to make her ascend back above the trees, but Shami was frightened of the bright flashes of light and the roar of the thunder. She flew jerkily between the trees as Ben held on for dear life. Amy felt in her pocket for the whistle. Perhaps if she whistled, Shami would understand the order and fly upwards again, but before she could put it to her lips, they passed under the branches of a huge tree and Shami swerved to one side. Ben managed to maintain his hold, but as Amy was reaching for the whistle, she was knocked to the side and completely lost her balance. Her legs swung away from the dragon, but somehow she managed to cling to one of Shami's spikes with her right hand and reach out for Ben's help with the other. She was barely able to breathe as she held out Shami's whistle. Ben managed to take it from her, whilst maintaining his balance, and quickly put it in his pocket. He grabbed hold of Amy's free hand and tried to pull her up onto Shami's back, but to his horror he could feel that she was slipping. He fought with all his might to hold on to her, terrified that they would both fall to the forest floor. He feared that he was losing his grip, and then, suddenly, Amy was gone!

Ben gasped as she fell through the branches and hit the ground; surely badly injured or worse. His chest tightened with fear as he looked down at the forest below, searching for her in the trees. Then he saw something move, and his hopes kindled as he saw her stand. However, his glee was short-lived when he glimpsed the Unicerons running through the trees towards her. He managed to kick Shami hard and she turned and started flying towards where Amy had fallen, but to Ben's dismay the Unicerons reached her first. They immediately pushed Amy to the ground and tied her hands behind her back. Other Unicerons started throwing spears at Ben and Shami, and one hit the dragon's tail and bounced off. Ben shouted for Amy, and could see that she was now standing and yelling helplessly back at them. He desperately wanted to help her, but knew it was a hopeless quest.

He looked sadly down at Amy, and understood from her frantic movements that she was telling him to flee. He felt sick in the pit of his stomach as he realised that he had no other option. If he stayed to help her, both Shami and he would surely be killed. Despair and guilt swept over him as he reached inside his pocket and found the whistle that Amy had passed to him. Shami immediately reacted to its sound and rose high into the sky, away from the flying spears and poor Amy. For one last time, Ben glanced down at her in complete despair, before flying off through the storm and into the distance.

Chapter 6

The Moonstone

Ben arrived back at the Citadel late that evening and found the Moonbeamers anxiously waiting for him at the main gate. When he saw them, he jumped down from Shami and ran towards them, trembling and shaking with grief.

"They have Amy… they have taken her!" he cried in despair.

He struggled to stay upright, and Tia helped him walk to a nearby bench.

"Who has Amy, Ben?" Hal asked, looking very concerned.

"The Unicerons! The thunder and lightning scared Shami and she tried to land in the wood, but there were Unicerons on the ground. Shami jerkily dodged some trees and Amy lost her balance. I tried to grab her and stop her from falling, honestly I did, but I couldn't hold on and she fell down into the trees. The branches broke her fall and then she started to run, but it was too late; the Unicerons had seen her. They caught her easily and then tied her hands behind her back. They saw me too and started throwing spears. Amy was shouting to me… shouting that I should go quickly. Please believe me, I didn't want to leave her but there was nothing I could do. If I had landed in the wood with Shami, they would have taken me as a hostage and killed Shami. Please, you have to help her… we cannot leave her with the Unicerons." Ben sobbed uncontrollably.

"Calm down, Ben. You did the right thing coming back here alone. Don't worry, we will think of a way to rescue your friend. Tia will take you to your room; there is nothing you can do for Amy in this shaken state. Go and rest and we will bring you some supper. Try and get some sleep and we will meet in the Great Hall at one o'clock in the morning."

"Why one o'clock in the morning?" asked Ben. "That's the middle of the night!"

"I have a plan, and all will be revealed later! Now go with Tia and try to get some rest."

Ben was woken just before one o'clock by a soft tapping on the chamber door. He jumped out of bed and dressed quickly. Tia waited for him outside, and they made their way down to the Great Hall. The council of senior Moonbeamers were already seated, so Ben took his place at the table.

"I'm sorry to disturb your sleep and meet at this early hour, but it is essential if my plan is to succeed," announced Hal. "I presume that Amy will have been taken to Cottisham Castle and handed over to the King. The Unicerons saw you, Ben, so they will now associate Amy with a Giddle. The King will want answers, so Amy is sure to be interrogated. However, they are unlikely to do this in the middle of the night, and this is where my plan comes into force. We will try and contact her using one of the moonstones."

"The moonstones!" gasped Ben. Why hadn't he thought of that?! Fresh hope swept over him instantly.

"We need to try this at night when hopefully she is alone," announced Hal. "If anyone were to see the moonstone glowing, our plan would be thwarted and the stone taken from her. I will try and contact her using my moonstone; all being well, she still has hers in her possession and will answer us."

Ben eagerly moved over to where Hal was sitting, and Hal started to rub the moonstone between his hands. As he rubbed, he closed his eyes and chanted Amy's name several times. Nothing happened for what seemed like several minutes, but then suddenly, Hal's stone began to glow. He opened his eyes as Ben stared at the stone, his hopes rising. It glowed around the edges, and the centre of the stone became hazy.

As the haze cleared, a face began to appear… Amy's face!

"Hello, Amy." Hal grinned. "I hope I didn't wake you?"

"I was just dozing and felt the stone burning in my pocket. I was beginning to worry that you had forgotten all about me. I contemplated trying to use the stone myself, but decided it would be safer to wait."

"We had to wait until night-time, to ensure that you were not being interrogated when we made contact. This is our only means of communication, so we do not want the stone discovered. Make sure you

70

keep it well hidden. I hope you have not been treated too badly. Where are you?"

"They have brought me to Numblebrook Island Prison!" declared Amy sadly.

Ben saw concerned looks from the Moonbeamers and realised that this was not the answer they were hoping for.

"First of all, they dragged me before the King. They know that I was with Ben, and they know that he is a Giddle. They threatened to torture me if I did not tell them where he's hiding, so I told them a lie! I told them that Ben has been hiding out in the caves at Spinnington Point. That's a good distance from here and I thought it would take them a good few days to check out my story. Whilst the King's guards investigate, I have been brought here to the prison. You need to help me before they discover that I've lied!"

"I'm not sure how we will be able to reach the island without being seen. The only dragon which is permitted entry is the King's red dragon which pulls his chariot. If we send Shami or another dragon, they will certainly be spotted."

"The King's chariot leaves Cottisham Castle to go to the island at seven o'clock each evening. It brings all new prisoners here, and also delivers supplies. The chariot then returns to the castle at eight o'clock in the morning, bringing back any prisoners with whom the King wishes to speak. At least two Unicerons from the King's guard accompany the chariot at all times," Amy whispered.

"Can you recall seeing anywhere on the chariot that somebody could possibly hide?" asked Hal optimistically.

"There is a storage area at the back, but the Unicerons regularly use this space. When travelling here, I placed my cloak on the floor by my feet and when I picked it up, I noticed that below the seat was a short curtain. I lifted the curtain and peeped underneath, but it was nothing but an empty space. If someone could board the chariot unnoticed, they could lie there unseen. However, the chariot is closely guarded and trying to board it without being noticed would be virtually impossible!"

"I could take one of my invisibility sweets and board without anyone seeing me! I think they usually work for around an hour, which would give me plenty of time to find my hiding spot" added Ben eagerly.

"But what about when you become visible again, Ben? It would be extremely dangerous!" advised Hal. "And you can't eat one sweet every hour, otherwise there would be none left for your return journey!"

"I could stay hidden beneath the seats so that nobody sees me. Once we reach the island, I can wait until nightfall, eat another sweet and then go searching for Amy. I'm sure there will be plenty of hiding places on the island should I need them. Don't worry, I can do this. Please trust me. Just help me get to Cottisham Castle and then leave the rest to me!"

"What about escaping from the island?" Hal asked with a concerned look in his eyes.

"I will find a way. I will keep in contact with you by using the moonstone if need be. When we arrive back at the castle we can stay hidden under the seats and whistle for Shami. All you need to do is make sure that Shami is nearby. The King will never know that the Moonbeamers are involved and hopefully, nobody will notice that Amy is missing until it is too late."

Hal looked at Ben doubtfully. "If you insist that this is what you want, then so be it. We will help you, Ben, but you must understand how dangerous this is going to be!"

"Does anyone have any better ideas?" asked Ben.

Only silence followed.

"Amy helped me when I first arrived in Numblebrook and now I need to return the gesture. It's my fault that she's in this mess in the first place, so my mind is made up! I will travel to Numblebrook Island Prison on the seven o'clock chariot tonight!"

Chapter 7

Numblebrook Island Prison

At two o'clock that afternoon, Ben, Hal and Ballin were ready to leave. They took Shami and Sissy and flew to some woodland located at a safe distance from Cottisham Castle. From here they walked for the remainder of the journey, keeping well hidden amongst the trees in the forest. As the castle came into view they stopped to rest.

"From here you will have to continue alone, Ben," said Hal. "You need to eat one of your invisibility sweets to ensure you are not seen. Then you should be able to walk straight into the castle grounds without anyone realising that you are there. The chariot leaves from just inside the castle gates at seven o'clock. Once you have climbed aboard, you need to hide yourself beneath the seat and make certain that the curtain is drawn around you. It is paramount that when your visibility returns, you stay well hidden. If anyone should discover your whereabouts, quickly swallow another sweet. But remember to use the sweets wisely; you only have a limited amount and will be in need of them again. We will retreat into the woodland, where we will camp for the night and await your return. If everything goes according to plan, we will expect you and Amy to be on the chariot when it returns here in the morning. Once the chariot has landed, stay hidden until everyone else has disembarked. You then need to whistle for Shami; we will make sure that she is ready to fly to you. Shami's flight into the castle grounds will surprise the guards. You and Amy will need to act very quickly and climb on her back before anyone notices what is happening. As soon as the Unicerons realise that this is a rescue mission, you will be in grave danger. Hopefully, if all goes to plan it will be too late for them to act!"

Ben took the jar of red sweets out of his pocket and unscrewed the lid. "Shower me with luck!" He grinned.

The Moonbeamers patted him on the shoulder and wished him all the best. Ben then popped one of the sweets into his mouth and within a few seconds his fingers started to tingle. The tingling sensation spread up his arms and into the rest of his body. He looked down at his legs as they began to turn hazy, and within a few seconds he was totally invisible.

"Can you still hear me?" he whispered, not sure whether being invisible also meant he could not be heard.

"Yes, we can still hear you, Ben. We just can't see you," answered Hal.

"Can you feel me?" asked Ben, worried that others might be aware he was present if he accidentally bumped into anything.

Hal held out his hand to where Ben was standing and waved it around. Ben looked down to where he knew his body was and watched Hal's hand moving straight through him.

"No, I cannot feel you!"

"Can you feel this?" asked Ben curiously, pinching Hal on the arm.

"Ouch!" Hal squealed softly in surprise.

A mischievous grin appeared on Ben's face. "I think I quite like being invisible. I could have lots of fun!"

"I'm sure you could," Hal smiled, "but I suggest you leave your fun for another time and begin your journey before the effects of the sweet wear off. You wouldn't like to become visible before you reach your hiding place, would you, Ben?"

"Very well, I'm going!" laughed Ben, before walking out of the trees and heading directly towards the castle.

As he approached, he was able to observe the castle in more detail and view it in all its splendour. He immediately understood why people referred to it as a palace. It was a huge building made of stone, with several turrets around its perimeter wall. Flags flew from every turret and archers were positioned on each. The drawbridge over the moat was the most majestic bridge he had ever seen; it reminded him of when he had visited Tower Bridge in London, though this bridge was decorated in gold. The large, beautiful castle gates were open, and sentries were posted on the bridge. Ben walked towards them feeling apprehensive, but he need not have worried: he was able to walk straight past them as they were totally unaware of his presence. He walked through the large golden gates and into the castle grounds. A wide cobbled path stretched the length of the courtyard up to the main doors of the castle. Stone pathways forked in various directions and ended at smaller doors in the castle walls. The grounds were full of flowers and trees in great abundance. Benches and other seating areas were scattered around, and many of the King's men were sitting, enjoying the early-evening sunshine. One of the paths led to a large stone circle, where the chariot waited. Ben began to walk towards it and studied every detail. The only area of the chariot which was covered by a roof was the rear compartment, which could be entered via a small door. The rest of the chariot was open-topped and contained several bench seats. Beneath the chariot were long metal runners, similar to those of a sledge that would be pulled along in the snow. It reminded Ben of Santa's sleigh in the movies, but this sleigh was not pulled by reindeer, for in front of the chariot stood the most enormous dragon that Ben had ever seen. It was red and had huge spiked wings which could span a whole football pitch. It was vicious-looking, and Ben wondered how on earth the King had managed to train such a beast. Amy had warned him that red dragons were dangerous, and Ben presumed that the King must have cast a spell on this dragon to make it his own. The dragon had what appeared to be a harness around its neck and body, with reins that stretched as far as the chariot. Ben crept past the dragon and climbed in. There were four rows of seats with a narrow aisle down the middle. At the front was a large chair, and Ben assumed that one of the King's guards would sit there to drive. Ben began to walk towards the rear of the chariot and immediately noticed a curtain which hung below the back row of seats. He bent down and peered behind it; Amy was right, it was just an empty space.

Ben heard voices approaching and noticed a group of around ten people shuffling towards him. Some were handcuffed and being led by the King's men. Ben quickly hid beneath the bench and closed the curtain. He listened to the party boarding and heard the guards shouting orders to their prisoners.

There were rustling sounds as people took their seats. Ben's spirits soared when he realised that nobody had chosen to sit on the back row where he was hiding.

"To Numblebrook Island Prison!" shouted one of the guards

Ben felt a sudden jerk and was thrust backwards as the dragon-drawn chariot rose into the sky. He heard the gasps of the prisoners as the carriage tilted to one side on its ascent. However, after a few initial bumps and jolts, the journey seemed relatively smooth and Ben began to relax.

About twenty minutes into the journey, he felt his fingers start to tingle and knew immediately what was happening. He looked down at his body and saw that it was becoming visible again. At first, he panicked and pulled the jar of sweets from his pocket, but then decided that he was hidden well enough and not in immediate need of one.

He was just beginning to relax when something caught his attention and he listened carefully. There were two prisoners sitting in the row in front of him, and for some reason, their voices sounded oddly familiar. He could not quite make out what they were saying as their words were muffled, but there was definitely a familiarity that Ben could not fathom. He felt a few more jolts and jerks, and then heard the scraping sound of the metal runners under the chariot as it came to a standstill. They had arrived.

"Numblebrook Island Prison. All dismount!"
shouted one of the guards.

Ben heard the prisoners pick up their scarce
belongings and start walking towards the front of the
chariot. Once again he heard a familiar voice, and
slowly pulled the curtain slightly to one side. There
was a gap just big enough for him to peep through,
and he glanced at the prisoners and counted six in all.
He was just about to move the curtain back in case he
was seen, but then something made him hesitate and

he stared in astonishment. One of the prisoners had turned to look behind him. It was Jacob! He climbed down from the chariot and Ben watched as he and Owen were led away in handcuffs.

Chapter 8
The Rescue

Ben waited beneath the bench for what seemed like a very long time. Night fell and everything was now dark. He thought about Jacob and Owen and how they must have followed him into this weird and magical land. He wondered whether the old hag had told them which passageway he had chosen, or whether it was just a coincidence that they had picked the same route. He also wondered how they had managed to pass her without paying ten noggings!

Although Owen and Jacob had been incredibly mean to him, he still felt a little sorry for them and wondered whether he should help. Could he leave them here on the island, locked away for a lifetime? Their families would be as worried as his own. Ben thought about it for a long time, unsure what to do.

He was a kind-hearted boy, and even though Jacob and Owen had been nasty to him, he didn't like the thought of leaving them here in this dreadful place.

Ben had an idea! The Moonbeamers had still not thought of how they were going to gain entry to the red dragon's lair without being seen. Their only plan so far was that Ben would eat a sweet and enter unnoticed, but he didn't like the thought of going in alone. Jacob and Owen were both Giddles and therefore, the red sweets would make them invisible too. His mind was made up: he would not enter the lair on his own; Jacob and Owen would enter too! As well as rescuing Amy, he would rescue Owen and Jacob, but there would be conditions and they would have to agree to help! Besides, what other option would they have?

Ben waited another couple of hours until everything was silent and checked his watch. It was two in the morning and Hal had told him that sunrise was around five o'clock. He ate one of the red sweets and immediately became invisible. He climbed out from under the seat and stretched his legs; he had been lying in the small space for several hours and his body ached. He quickly climbed down from the chariot and looked at the sleeping dragon, still in harness. It did not stir, and Ben headed off in the same direction that the prisoners had been taken.

As he walked, he looked around and decided that

this was probably the strangest place he had ever visited. Where the island ended, there was nothing but sky and stars. There were no railings or other barriers; you could just walk straight off the edge and fall into the sky. Ben shuddered. No wonder prisoners never escaped from this awful place!

The path led to a doorway where a bored-looking sentry was on duty. He sat reading a book, and Ben walked straight past him without being seen. He crept along a hallway until he reached a scruffy reception area. A sleeping guard was slumped in a wooden chair at the desk. Ben walked over to a large metal board, where hundreds of large brass keys were dangling. Each key hung next to a number, and Ben presumed these related to which cell they would unlock. He wondered which one would open Amy's cell, and searched around for any clues. He noticed a drawer in the desk and tried to open it without waking the snoring guard. The Uniceron stirred in his sleep and Ben leapt quickly backwards, but to his relief the guard continued to snore. He felt around inside the drawer and found a map of the prison, showing each numbered cell. He also found a little book, and felt a stab of excitement as he realised that it identified who occupied each room. He quickly scanned the names and found Amy's written by Cell 102. Further down the list, he discovered that Jacob and Owen were both in Cell 151. He placed the book carefully back in the drawer and closed it quietly, taking the map with him.

A long flight of concrete steps led him to a large landing, with passageways leading off in three different directions. He studied the map and crept down the centre passage towards Cell 102. Ben heard wails coming from behind one of the doors and hurried along, eager to escape the awful high-pitched shrieks. Eventually he came to Amy's cell and studied the sliding panel on the wide metal door. He released a catch and the panel slid to one side, revealing a small, square hole. Ben looked through the gap, searching for Amy in the darkness.

"Amy, Amy. Are you in there?" he muttered softly.

A figure in the corner started to stir and then sat up.

"Amy, is that you?"

"Ben?" whispered a small voice.

"Yes, it's me!"

Amy leapt up in delight and ran over to the doorway. Joy overwhelmed her as she bent her head down to the hole and peered through.

"You won't be able to see me," murmured Ben, "I've taken one of my invisibility sweets."

"Thank you so much for coming to get me. It's awful here, I've been so afraid. Did anyone see you?"

"No, I ate a sweet before I climbed aboard the chariot and then I hid under the seats, just like you said. I stayed hidden until well into the night and then crept into the prison. The guard on reception was asleep and I managed to steal the key."

Ben felt in his pocket and took out the two cell keys. He looked at their numbers and quickly inserted one into the lock and opened the door. "I'll go ahead and check each passageway. You need to make sure you are well hidden. I have also discovered that two boys from my class at school are locked away here too!"

"What, you mean there are two more Giddles on the island?" asked Amy in amazement.

"Yes! They must have followed me through the passageway and into this land. They aren't my friends, but I can't leave them here. I'm going to help rescue them, but in return they must help us to solve the riddle. I will need you to help as they won't be able to see me."

"Do you know where they are?" replied Amy eagerly.

"Yes, they're in Cell 151; I have the key here. We need to lock your cell behind us, otherwise someone might notice it is open and realise you are gone."

Amy stepped out of the cell and Ben locked the door quickly.

"What time do they normally come and check on you in the morning?"

"They bring breakfast to our rooms at about eight o'clock," answered Amy in a hushed voice.

"That's good – the chariot leaves at seven, so hopefully, we will already be back at the castle before anyone notices you are missing."

They crept down the passageway back towards the main landing, and Ben peeped around the corner to check the coast was clear. He gave Amy a little tug and they sneaked towards Cell 151.

They eventually came to the large metal door, and Ben released the catch and slid the viewing panel to one side. He could see two silhouettes sleeping in the corner.

"Jacob, Owen, can you hear me?" he whispered.

One of the silhouettes stirred and sat bolt upright.

"Yes. Who is it? What do you want?" answered Jacob nervously as he tugged at Owen's shirt. "Someone is at the door!" he whispered to his fellow prisoner.

"It's me, Ben."

"Ben! Is that really you? What are you doing here? Have they taken you prisoner too?" gasped Jacob, quickly moving towards the door and peering through the hole. "I can't see you!"

"You can't see me because I'm invisible!" replied Ben mischievously.

"Please don't tease us," sniffled Jacob. "I know we were horrible to you. We didn't mean to be; we just thought it was funny. But this is serious, we are prisoners. We're scared and we want to go home!"

Ben giggled. He found it amusing that he finally had the upper hand over the two bullies. "I'm not teasing you," he answered, "I really am invisible. The old lady in the cave gave me some magic sweets. I came

here to save my friend Amy; it's just a coincidence that I found you both here."

Amy moved over to the hole in the doorway, so that Jacob and Owen could see her. They stared at her in disbelief through the gap.

"Hello, I'm Amy," she whispered, pushing her arm through the hole. Jacob and Owen shook her hand in stunned silence.

Ben had every intention of helping the boys, but first he thought he would have a little fun of his own. After all, he wasn't going to let Jacob and Owen off the hook that easily!

"Well, it was nice bumping into you again. We'll be off now. See ya!" he said in a very serious voice, pulling Amy away from the door and starting to head back towards the stairs.

"You can't leave us here!" cried Owen, sobbing uncontrollably.

"Where are you going? Please, you have to help us!" pleaded Jacob.

Ben and Amy walked back towards the door and Ben smiled to himself.

"And just why should I help you?" he whispered. "After all, you were calling me names the last time I saw you!"

"We are sorry, really we are. Like I said, it was just a joke. Please forgive us. You can't leave us here. Please!" Owen begged.

"Let me think…" Ben said, finding the whole situation particularly amusing. "If I help rescue you, will you help me in return?"

"Anything, we will do anything! Just let us out and I give you my word," sobbed Jacob.

"I am trying to locate the passageway to find my way home," said Ben. "The Moonbeamers are helping me, but first they have to overthrow the King."

Jacob and Owen looked at each other in bewilderment.

"To do this we need to solve a riddle, and this involves some dangerous tasks. I need you both to help us on these missions. After all, the outcome will benefit you too, as it means finding our way home."

"Yes, we'll do it, I promise you. We'll do anything you ask!" cried Jacob.

"OK," replied Ben, "but you had better keep your promise!"

He unlocked the cell and Jacob and Owen quickly slid out before Ben relocked the door.

"This way," he whispered, giving Amy a little tug.

They made their way back along the corridor and down the stairs. At the bottom of the steps, Ben told the others to stay hidden whilst he quietly returned the keys and map. He found the Uniceron still snoring and quickly replaced the items without disturbing him. He whistled for the others to follow and they all sneaked past the guard, crawling on all fours behind the reception desk.

The guard at the main entrance was still reading, and Ben quickly thought of a plan.

"Do you know the way back to the chariot from here?" he whispered.

"I think so," replied Amy in a hushed voice.

"Good, then I have an idea. I will go ahead as the guard can't see me. I will head down the side of the building, away from the chariot. I will do something to alert the guard, and hopefully he will go to investigate. This should give you just enough time to creep past the entrance and reach the chariot before he sees you. Remember to move quietly, though, as you do not want to wake the dragon. Once you are safe, I will come and join you on the chariot."

"Be careful!" whispered Amy.

Ben sneaked off down the corridor in the direction of the main entrance. The guard was still engrossed in a book, oblivious to him walking past. Ben turned right and followed the pathway leading to the rear of the building. He frantically looked around, searching for something he could use to distract the guard. He found an old wooden barrel lying on its side in the grass, picked it up and threw it against the stone wall of the prison. It made an enormous bang and then rolled along the cobbles with a loud creaking sound.

The guard jumped up and immediately pulled out his sword. He quickly followed the pathway to the right, looking for the source of the strange noise. Amy and the boys heard the noise and knew that this was their cue. Amy motioned to the boys to follow her. They crept to the main entrance and looked in both directions; the guard was nowhere to be seen. They ran as quickly as possible towards the chariot, where the dragon was still sleeping soundly. They sneaked aboard and hid beneath the seats, with the curtain hiding them from view.

Ben saw that the others had made it safely to the chariot and went to follow. Suddenly he felt his fingers start to tingle and knew immediately that within a few seconds he would be visible again. He could hear the guard's footsteps heading back towards the front of the building. He needed to run. His heart pounded with fear as he looked down at his body and realised his legs were beginning to reappear. The sound of the guard's boots was getting louder, and he looked back as he ran. He reached the chariot, jumped aboard and hid beneath the side rail, just as the guard came into view back at his post outside the prison. Ben peeped through the railings, holding his breath. The guard sat back down in his chair and Ben's heart leapt in relief. He lay on his stomach and slithered across the chariot floor towards the curtain.

They lay huddled together for a long time and eventually, they heard people boarding the chariot. Guards were shouting orders and three prisoners were brought on board. The prisoners were being taken to the King, but the reason was unclear. They listened carefully to the guards' conversations and remained hopeful that their absence had not yet been discovered. At precisely seven o'clock, orders were given to commence the flight and they were thrust backwards with the force of the chariot climbing into the air. They knew that the flight down to Cottisham

Castle would take approximately thirty minutes, and thus they would arrive at 7.30am.

With five minutes of the journey remaining, Ben handed Jacob and Owen a red sweet each and they took them gratefully, eager not to be found. All three boys ate the sweets and within seconds they were invisible. Amy felt a little apprehensive that she was now the only one who could be seen.

The chariot landed smoothly and Ben listened to the passengers disembarking. He peeped through the curtain and watched the three handcuffed prisoners being led away by the guards. Ben moved out of his hiding place, still invisible to anyone who might be observing. Jacob and Owen followed him, but Amy remained where she was, hidden from prying eyes. Ben looked around and could see guards on the castle wall. Nothing was out of the ordinary and everything seemed relaxed and undisturbed.

"Are you ready for me to whistle for Shami?" he whispered to Amy.

"Yes! Let's just get this over with," answered Amy, eager to escape.

Ben took the whistle from his pocket and put it to his lips. He blew with all his might and the high-pitched sound could be heard all around the castle grounds. The guards looked around in confusion, unsure what the sound was or where it had come from. An eerie silence followed as they stood still and listened. Then, out of nowhere, Shami appeared, flying high over the castle wall and descending into the grounds beside the chariot. The three boys climbed quickly onto her back, unseen by the Unicerons. Ben shouted to Amy and she emerged from her hiding place and fled towards Shami, holding out her hands to be helped onto the dragon's back.

The Unicerons saw her immediately, and angry voices could be heard as the guards realised this was a rescue mission. They ran towards Shami with spears raised, and an alarm sounded. Ben gave the dragon a quick kick with his heels and she took off into the sky. Arrows were fired from the castle walls, and the four children clung on to Shami as tightly as they could. She jerked as a loud, deep booming noise was heard, and Ben looked down in horror as he saw the Unicerons loading a cannon. Another huge boom filled the air as the cannon was fired, and Ben just about managed to steer Shami clear of its path. She sped through the sky, flying faster than Ben had ever known her to do, away from the castle, out across the morning sky, carrying four very weary but ecstatic youngsters away from danger.

Chapter 9

Glamoran

The children arrived back at the Citadel later that day, where they met with Hal and Ballin who had returned from the wood with Sissy. Amy was thrilled to be back and ran excitedly into Tia's arms. Ben explained what had happened on the island and introduced Owen and Jacob to the Moonbeamers. Owen, in particular, seemed pleased to be in safe company and regularly expressed his gratitude to Ben. He was a small boy for his age, with pale-blue eyes, red hair and freckles. Jacob, on the other hand, was a tall, stern-looking boy with brown hair and brown eyes. He didn't express the same gratitude as Owen had done, and Ben wasn't sure whether he could be totally trusted.

"Well done on your mission, Ben!" declared Hal, smiling. "It was a very brave act to undertake, going to

Numblebrook Island Prison and rescuing young Amy and your fellow Giddles. You should be extremely proud of yourself. It was a very dangerous mission and I have to admit, I was not overly confident that you would succeed. But I am pleased to say you have proved me wrong. Your friends owe you a great deal and I'm sure that they will be forever indebted to you."

Amy and Owen expressed their thanks and smiled, but Jacob just nodded silently, his eyes hard and scornful.

"Whilst I was away, did you fathom out where the red dragon's lair is?" asked Ben, feeling a little embarrassed with all the praise and wanting to change the subject.

"The senior members of the council have been doing a lot of research, Ben," Hal answered. He took out the blue coin that they had found in the Gothic Well and placed it on the table. "It appears that this coin is made from turquoise, and we believe that this may be a clue as to the whereabouts of the cave. According to the ancient books, there was once a small, remote mining community up in the hills near the village of Glamoran, far in the east. It was here that they mined for turquoise, and it was once a thriving business. However, one day the mine ran dry and there was no more turquoise to be found, so the mines were abandoned. There are tales that a red dragon dwelled in the nearby caves, close to this community. The dragon was extremely volatile and ferocious, and the villagers lived in fear of their lives. Once the mine had run dry, they were more than happy to distance themselves from the dragon and quickly moved away to more densely populated areas where other trades could be found. Red dragons can live for many hundreds of years and it is possible that this dragon still resides there. This is where we shall begin our search."

"What will we do once we get there?" Amy shivered.

Hal read out the verse from the riddle:

Hidden in the caves
Is the red dragon's lair.
Count the spikes on his back;
Beware of the bear.

"The verse says we have to count the spikes on the dragon's back. To do this with any certainty, we will have to be very close to the dragon. Red dragons are extremely dangerous and hard to kill, so we will have to count his spikes whilst he sleeps."

"Is that where we help?" muttered Owen nervously. "Do we need to eat some of the invisibility sweets before we enter the dragon's lair?"

"Unfortunately, I can think of no other way," answered Hal. "We will stay close by. We still have some use of the old magic, but we will try and avoid using it as it may alert the King. However, if any of you are in any danger we will use the magic without delay. This should stun the dragon long enough for you to escape from the cave."

"What does *Beware of the bear* mean?" asked Owen.

"We are not sure," answered Hal. "Bears have been extinct in this land for a very long time. Hopefully this bear no longer exists, but we need to be on the lookout just in case."

"When do we leave?" asked Ben impatiently, eager to solve the riddle so that he could go home.

"We will depart first thing tomorrow. After this morning's rescue, the King will be monitoring the skies for dragons, especially Shami. It will be safer to travel by horseback."

Amy looked disappointed that Shami would not be accompanying them, and Ben smiled at her reassuringly.

"Do not worry, Amy, Shami will be well looked after by the Moonbeamers. She is safe here," added Hal, sensing Amy's disappointment.

The Giddles, Amy, Hal, Shadrack, Ballin and Josiah met early the next morning to begin their journey on horseback. Tia accompanied them, and Amy seemed pleased that she was no longer the only female in the group. The hills of Glamoran were far to the east and the party travelled for several days, stopping only to rest and sleep. They travelled mainly through wooded areas, and picked routes where they were unlikely to be spotted.

After five days on the road they eventually came to the deserted and dilapidated village of Glamoran. They rode their horses through what remained of the streets and observed the shabby buildings as they passed. Faded signs that were barely readable remained above some of the doorways and shop windows. One read *Glamoran Inn* and another *Groceries of Glamoran*. Ben imagined that this was once a lively and thriving village, and felt sad that it had become a derelict and deserted array of buildings and overgrowth.

They tied up the horses and continued to walk along the dusty, narrow streets to get a closer look at what remained of the town. Suddenly Ben thought he saw something out of the corner of his eye. As he focused, he saw something disappear around the corner of a building and head off down the cobbled side road. He ran over to the building and peeped around the corner. He was startled to see an old lady with a walking stick leaning against an old gas street light. She turned to look at Ben, and he immediately recognised her as the hag he had met at Labyrinth Junction in the cave! Ben gasped in surprise. Without saying a word, the old witch beckoned for him to follow her and started to hobble down the street. Ben quickly turned to look for the others and saw them peering into an old shop window.

"Quickly, come here!" he shouted eagerly.

"What is it, Ben?" yelled Hal, as they ran towards him.

"The old witch from the cave, she's here!" gasped Ben. He turned to look back towards her, but to his surprise she had vanished. The road was empty and quiet except for a large black raven which sat on top of a street light, squawking loudly.

"Where is she?" asked Amy, looking round apprehensively.

"She was here a second ago, I swear she was!" cried Ben. "She can't have walked off that quickly. She was hobbling with a walking stick and there is nowhere for her to hide!"

"Maybe your eyes are playing tricks on you, Ben," said Hal softly. "You have had a tough few days and you are tired."

"My eyes weren't playing tricks. I know what I saw; she was here!" Ben protested.

The raven let out a piercing squawk and they all looked up. It then flew along the lane and landed on another street light a few feet away. As it turned to look at them, it let out another high shriek.

"It wants us to follow it!" gasped Ben, as he ran in the direction of the flying raven.

Amy and Hal followed Ben as the others ran back to where the horses had been tethered. The raven flew from light to light waiting for Ben to catch up. He entered a wooded area and stumbled across the roots of large trees as he tried to keep up with the strange bird.

Eventually, they came to an old wooden hut and the raven flew straight through the open doorway with Ben, Amy and Hal in pursuit. It glided across the room and landed on a window opening which contained no glass. Ben ran to the window and looked out. To his amazement he was no longer looking at the wood but staring straight across a quarry, a huge quarry thousands of feet deep! It looked like a massive, circular, empty basin with steep, rocky sides. An old rusted shaft could be seen at the far side, and Ben knew that this must have once been a working mine. An occasional tree had grown along the steep sides and overgrowth filled the bottom of the basin. The wooden building was probably an old lookout point for the mineworkers.

The raven gave a high-pitched squawk and flew off the window ledge into the air above the quarry. As Ben watched it fly into the distance, his attention was diverted to something else approaching through the sky. At first he thought that it was a huge bird, but as it got nearer, he realised that this beast was far too large to be a bird. He began to make out its reddish colour and its shape, with the most enormous wings that he had ever seen and an extremely long, jagged tail. Ben, Amy and Hal gasped in horror as the creature opened its huge jaws and blew out a great, glittering ball of fire. The dragon glided through the air towards the far side of the basin and landed gracefully on the rock face. It turned to look back across the quarry before swooping into a large cave and disappearing from sight.

"I think we have found our red dragon!" Hal stated uneasily.

The others looked across the basin of the quarry in fear.

Chapter 10
The Red Dragon's Lair

The horses were left to graze in the wood close to the lookout hut whilst the group considered their next move. The dragon's cave was high up on the opposite side of the quarry, and to reach it on foot quickly without being seen would be virtually impossible.

"I think we need the help of Shami or one of the other dragons," said Amy. "I know you said it was dangerous, Hal, as you thought that Shami could easily be spotted, but I think we have no other option."

"Maybe you are right, Amy," agreed Hal. "I can't think of any other way we can reach the dragon's cave safely either. It would take us a long time to climb the cliff face and the risk of being seen by the red dragon would be too great. I will use the moonstone to communicate with the Moonbeamers back at the Citadel and arrange for Shami and one of the other dragons to be flown here. The journey by air will only be a few hours, so they should reach us by early evening. Dragons normally sleep at night, so once darkness has fallen, we shall make our move."

"What's the plan?" asked Owen nervously.

"You, Ben and Jacob will each eat one of the red sweets," replied Hal. "Once you are invisible, we will fly over to the cave with the dragons. Amy and Tia, you will wait here with the horses and keep a lookout, just in case the King has his spies around. Ballin, Josiah and I will position ourselves outside the cave in case the dragon wakes. Hopefully, it will continue to sleep. Ben, Jacob and Owen, you will enter the cave and search for the red dragon. Once you have found it, you will need to count the number of spikes down its back and along its tail. You must do this very carefully, as there is no room for error. Although you will be invisible, you need to tread as quietly as possible, as it is imperative that you do not wake the dragon. And remember, the riddle refers to a bear. I have thought long and hard about this and unfortunately cannot make any sense of it. If by some miracle bears still exist, one would surely not dwell in such a place. But even so, make sure to remain alert. Does anyone have any questions?"

"The dragon will not be able to see us," Owen shivered, "but what if it can smell us?"

The group fell silent. Nobody seemed to have considered this, and a chill went through them.

"If the dragon wakes and you are in any danger, you need to shout for us immediately. We will wield some of the old magic if necessary. I don't really want to do this as it may alert the King to our whereabouts, but your safety is paramount and I will always put that first."

Jacob remained silent and didn't look particularly happy with the arrangements. Owen half-smiled, and Ben gave him a pat of encouragement.

"Don't worry, boys, we will be fine!" he laughed, although he could feel his heart thudding. But if doing this meant he would help to solve the riddle and thus find his way home, then he was determined. If this was the only way, so be it.

Shami and Sissy arrived early that evening with Kondo, one of Hal's aides. He was a hard-working and reliable Moonbeamer, whom Hal trusted with his life. Amy was delighted to be reunited with Shami, and the gentle dragon licked her face tenderly.

The group prepared for their task and everyone ensured that they had everything they needed. Ben checked he still had the moonstone in his possession before passing a red sweet to both Owen and Jacob.

"Before you eat the sweet, Ben, I think you should take this," interrupted Hal. He handed Ben the turquoise coin that they had found in the ancient well.

Ben took the coin and turned it over in his hands. "I thought that this was just to guide us to the dragon's lair?"

"Indeed, I am quite certain that this is true, but I feel that you should take it, just in case. I do not envisage that you will need it for anything."

Ben put the coin in his pocket and turned to the others. "Right, are we ready?" he asked.

"As ready as we will ever be!" replied Owen hesitantly.

"Good luck, boys!" said Amy in encouragement.

Ben popped the sweet into his mouth and immediately began to feel the tingling sensation spread through his arms and legs. Owen and Jacob followed suit, and they too felt the sweet begin to take effect. Within moments all three boys were invisible, and one by one they climbed onto Shami's back. Hal, Ballin and Josiah mounted Sissy and they all rose up into the sky and flew towards the red dragon's lair.

The two dragons landed on the small rocky platform at the front of the cave. Hal checked that they had all safely dismounted and then signalled to Amy and Tia back at the lookout point in the distance. The dragons took to the air, flying back in the direction from which they had come.

"Are you ready?" Hal asked softly.

Fear assailed the Giddles, but they ackowledged that they were ready and stepped into the cave entrance apprehensively. They used a small lantern to light the way. The floor was quite uneven and they had to tread carefully to stop themselves from tripping over. The roof seemed very high as the cave opened up into a huge, circular dome. They could see no sign of the dragon and continued to creep further into the dark. The children whispered to each other in encouragement as they walked deeper into the gloomy, rocky chamber.

Occasionally they could hear a soft tapping noise, like the sound of something being knocked lightly against the rocky wall. The noise became steadily louder as they walked deeper into the cave. Eventually, they spotted the outline of something huge and forbidding only a few feet in front of them, and Ben felt an overwhelming sense of dread overcome him. As they approached, they heard the terrifying snoring sound of the dragon's deep breathing. Its nostrils flared and occasionally it would slap its enormous tail against the rocky floor. They slowly approached, and Ben shone his light towards the huge, frightening creature. They could now see the dragon's body in detail and make out each huge spike along his gigantic, scaly back.

"Let's count the spikes as quickly as we can and get out of here!" whispered Owen shakily.

"We should count in our heads and then check that we all have the same number," added Ben quietly. He slowly shone the lantern towards the dragon's spikes, but to their horror it unexpectedly stirred

and lifted its huge, frightful head high into the air. The boys jumped backwards in shock and fear as its skull hit the floor once more. Thankfully, the dragon continued to sleep. Ben carefully returned the light to the dragon's spikes and slowly and methodically began to count. When he had finished he repeated his task, wanting to be certain that he had not made any errors.

"How many did you count?" whispered Owen from somewhere within the cave.

"Nineteen," answered Ben. "What about you?"

"Great, that's what I counted too!" murmured Owen.

"What about you, Jacob? How many did you count?" asked Ben softly.

There was only silence.

"Jacob, where are you?" asked Ben.

There was no reply.

"Jacob!" muttered Owen, a little too loudly.

An eerie silence followed, but then the dragon slowly began to stir! The two boys froze, and Ben felt the hair on his arms stand on end. The dragon lifted its ugly head into the air and, to their horror, slowly opened its eyes. Fear and numbness infused the boys' bodies. In despair Ben dropped the lantern and the dragon quickly swung round its head and stared in their direction with a ferocious look in its evil eyes. Ben stayed glued to the spot, knowing that he was invisible and praying that the dragon was unaware of their presence. He didn't want to do anything else to attract its attention, and silently held his breath in anticipation. The dragon looked straight towards him and seemed unable to see either him or Owen. But as Ben regained his composure, the dragon slowly began to twitch its nose!

"It can smell us!" whispered Owen in terror.

The dragon swiftly rose to its feet and started to make a terrifying roaring noise. It opened its mouth and blew out a large, dazzling, bright plume of fire.

"*Run!*" shouted Ben as he turned to flee towards the cave opening.

Ben and Owen ran for their lives, their hearts in their throats. The dragon leapt around the cave, trying to locate them using its strong sense of smell. It turned its head back towards them, twitching its nostrils, sniffing them out. Without warning it sent a huge ball of fire hurtling across the cave. The heat was intense and the boys flung themselves backwards against the rear wall to stop themselves being badly burnt. As Ben looked down he realised he was no longer invisible. He looked over at Owen and saw that he too was staring down at his body in absolute horror.

"The fire! It's made us visible again!" cried out Ben. "The witch warned me about heat, but I had forgotten all about it!"

Owen tried to answer, but panic assailed him as he saw the dragon plodding towards them, roaring wildly. The boys had their backs up against the wall and there was nowhere for them to run. Ben noticed a small stone on the floor, picked it up and threw it past the dragon to the far side of the cave. The stone made a loud, sharp noise as it hit the far wall and the dragon immediately turned towards the sound. Ben grabbed Owen's arm and quickly pulled him round the side of the chamber, trying to make his way towards the exit. The dragon scanned the cave to locate where the stone had landed and picked it up in its terrible jaws. It swung its head to one side and flung the stone with all its might across the chamber, just missing poor Owen. The dragon roared in anger at being tricked, and stomped towards the terrified boys as it sent more fireballs hurtling across the cave. Again, its huge, spiked tail rose into the air and started to swoop towards them. They closed their eyes, bracing themselves for the impact, fear hitting them like icy water.

But then, slowly, time seemed to stand still. They heard chanting, and cautiously opened their eyes. The dragon's tail was still heading towards them, but it was as if they were in a dream and the tail was moving in slow motion. Then, from behind the dragon, they saw Hal, sword in hand, shouting and chanting unknown foreign words that they could not understand. As the dragon's tail moved slowly towards them, Ben waited for the impact. But then, the beast seemed to crumble and disintegrate before their very eyes! Like a piece of glass, the dragon was shattering in front of them. Thousands of tiny fragments fell to the floor until there was just a heap of particles on the ground. Standing beside it was Hal, breathing deeply and looking exhausted. He looked at Ben and Owen before collapsing to the floor.

Ballin and Josiah ran into the cave to help him and check he was still conscious.

"I heard the dragon wake and came to your aid," Hal whispered weakly. "The King will know we have used magic to destroy the red dragon; he will be able to sense it from many miles away. We have to make haste and leave quickly."

"Here, hold on to my arm," said Ballin. "Josiah and I will help you out of the cave. Ben and Owen, you go ahead and whistle for the dragons."

Ben turned to leave, but as he did so, something on the rear wall of the cave caught his attention. This part of the chamber had previously been obscured by the sleeping dragon, but now Ben was looking at what appeared to be an ancient caveman drawing. He held up his lantern and, to his astonishment, realised it was an engraving of a bear.

"Look!" he shouted to his friends. "It's an engraving of a bear on the wall. I wonder whether this is the bear in the riddle?"

With interest, the others quickly looked over to where he was pointing.

"Be careful, Ben," said Ballin. "The riddle says, *Beware of the bear*. Perhaps this is some kind of trick!"

Ben took no notice, too interested in the strange drawing etched into the wall. He hurried over and touched it eagerly. A very sharp instrument must have been required to make the engraving, as it was etched deep into the rock. As he moved his fingertips across it, he felt a small, round hole. He shone the lantern towards it and to his surprise noticed some writing on the wall.

"Look, there's a small crevice on the top of the bear's back with some writing by it!" he exclaimed in excitement before reading aloud:

Insert the coin
And stand well back.
Those with courage
Will find the map.

"Do you think it means the turquoise coin from the well?" asked Josiah inquisitively.

Ben quickly took the coin from his pocket and held it up to the circular crevice in the wall. "It would fit perfectly!" he replied excitedly. "It must mean this coin. The picture of the bear on the coin exactly matches the engraving on the wall." He stepped forward, ready to insert the coin into the hole.

"Wait!" cried out Hal. "This could be a trick. The riddle says, *Beware of the bear*, and the writing on the wall warns us to stand well back. I'm not sure that this is a very clever idea!"

"We need to take that risk," advised Josiah. "If the rhyme on the wall states the truth, then we could find a map which might guide us to the Enchanter's Orb. The King's men will be on their way here as we speak; the magic you used will have exposed us to them. If there is a map here we need to locate it before they arrive, otherwise they will surely destroy it."

"Very well," replied Hal hesitantly. "But we need to do this carefully. The riddle advises us to stand well back. There must be a reason for this!"

"I am happy to take the risk whilst the rest of you stand well clear. Ben, Amy and Owen have taken the greater risks on this quest so far. Now I can play my part, and you are too weak, Hal."

Hal was quiet for a few moments, and the rest of the group waited for his response.

"All right Josiah, but only if you are sure you want to do this."

Josiah nodded as the rest of the party moved back towards the cave entrance. "Here goes!" he stated nervously.

"Remember to jump clear as soon as you have slotted the coin into the hole," replied Hal.

Josiah held the coin up to the crevice and slowly inserted it into the slot. He jumped back and waited, but nothing happened.

"Perhaps you haven't put it in far enough?" cried out Ben.

Josiah stepped forward and pushed the coin with his finger. As he did so, he felt it click into something inside the wall. Immediately a loud rumbling could be heard and the whole cave started to shake violently. Tons of huge, sharp pieces of rock from the ceiling crashed to the floor, shattering into thousands of tiny shards. Sharp debris flew in several directions, cutting into their skin as it was sent spinning across the chamber. A huge dust cloud filled the cave, making it difficult for them to breathe, and the group began to cough. As the dust slowly began to clear, they looked in disbelief at the rocky mounds which had fallen to the floor of the cave.

"The bear! It's gone!" shouted Josiah in amazement. A huge, gaping hole had appeared in the rock where the engraving had been. Josiah hurried over to the hole and shone his lantern deep inside. He saw something within and immediately pulled out a rolled-up piece of card tied with red ribbon. As he rolled out the scroll, he stared in excitement. "It's a map showing where the wise old man's cottage is!"

A wave of delight momentarily passed through the group.

"Fantastic, Josiah! Now let's get out of here before anything untoward happens," replied Hal.

"What about Jacob? We don't know where he is!" exclaimed Owen.

"I have a feeling we will find him outside the cave," replied Hal. "He was probably too scared to enter and, as he was invisible, he probably thought that he could get away with it!"

"You mean you think he deliberately let me and Ben come in here alone?"

"It was a very brave thing for you both to do, Owen. Don't hold it against him too much. Not everyone is as courageous as you and Ben have been. It takes someone very brave to come here and risk their life."

The group walked across the cave towards the entrance and out onto the high ledge into the moonlight. Sure enough, there was Jacob crouching down at the corner of the ridge. He was no longer invisible, and sat shaking and weeping.

"I'm sorry!" he cried. "I just couldn't bring myself to enter the dragon's cave."

"You're a coward!" shouted Owen. "I always looked up to you and thought you were the coolest in the class. But you let me and Ben go in there alone. You're a wimp, that's what you are!"

"Now, now, boys," exclaimed Hal. "The important thing is that we are all safe and we have the map. We should put this behind us; I'm sure Jacob is sorry for what he did and will make it up to both of you... don't you agree, Jacob? Now let's whistle for the dragons and get out of here!"

Owen glared at Jacob in absolute fury.

Chapter 11

Wimble

The party spent the next few days riding through the forests, mountains and open valleys of Numblebrook, making their way to the village near to where the wise old man resided. As before, they decided not to risk flying in case they were spotted by the King's guards. The Moonbeamers who had accompanied the dragons to the turquoise mines would fly them back to the Citadel and await further instructions.

The map guided them to a small village called Shnuggleton. Amy had stopped at this village many times in the past with her parents, when selling crops at the local market. Since her parents' deaths she had visited the village with Shami and said that the people were warm and welcoming and could be trusted. They hated the King and his men.

They reached Shnuggleton early one evening after a long day's ride. As they approached the village, children ran out to welcome them and Amy jumped down from her horse and ran over to greet her friends. Like Amy, all the children had bright blonde hair and big blue eyes.

She took the party to a local inn where the landlady, a chubby, jolly woman called Ruby, welcomed them. Ruby asked her stable hand to take care of the horses and cleared a table for Amy and her friends. The inn was quite busy, but nobody seemed to pay much attention to them. Ruby brought them all stew served with hot, crusty bread, and the Moonbeamers welcomed the large jug of ale which was brought to the table.

"What brings you to these parts? It's been a good few months since we have had any Moonbeamers passing through. And your friends certainly don't look like they are from the area!" said Ruby, looking suspiciously at Ben, Jacob and Owen.

"My friends are not from these parts!" replied Amy. "Anyhow, we are trying to help the Moonbeamers find a wise old man who lives nearby. He may have some information which could help win back the realm for the true heirs of this land – the Moonbeamers."

"Well, I wish you luck!" replied Ruby. "This land was a much happier place before that cruel King Ados and his father came to power. We used to get lots of passing trade back in those days, but now people are too afraid to travel and sell their goods."

"We are told that a wise old man lives in a cottage in the woods just north of this village. Do you know of such a man?" asked Hal.

"I know everyone who lives within fifty miles of this village, but I do not know of any wise old man," replied Ruby. "Are you sure you have come to the right place?"

Hal laid the map on the table and Ruby studied it carefully, looking closely at where the wise old man's house was drawn on the scroll.

"The cottage the map is referring to is only a mile or so north of here," she advised. "But the man who lives there is a hermit called Wimble and he's definitely not a wise old man... indeed, quite the opposite. He very occasionally comes into the village for groceries, but only when he has to. The rest of the time he never leaves his house. The children hide when he wanders into the village. He's a strange old thing, and certainly of unsound mind. He talks complete nonsense."

"Maybe there is some logic to his madness?" suggested Hal.

"I very much doubt it!" answered Ruby, laughing. "He's as mad as mad can be! Go and visit him and I'm sure you will agree. That's if you can get through his front door; he doesn't like visitors! Once I offered to arrange for his groceries to be delivered to him, but he will not allow anyone near his cottage. Even the children do not dare to go within a hundred yards of his home!"

"Are you sure that the map couldn't be referring to someone else who lives nearby?" asked Hal hopefully.

"Wimble's cottage is the only house in that part of the wood," replied Ruby, shaking her head.

"Then we shall go and visit him tomorrow," replied Hal. "He is our only hope!"

That night, Ruby accommodated her guests at the inn. Ben was grateful to sleep in a comfortable bed for once rather than on the rough forest floor. The next morning Ruby fed them a hearty breakfast and arranged for their horses to be fed and saddled. Josiah, Owen and Jacob would wait at the inn, whilst the others visited Wimble alone, fearing that too many of them would unsettle him.

They set off on their short journey and found the cottage easily. It was an old, ramshackle stone cottage with rotten windows and chipped paint. Smoke rose from the chimney. The curtains were drawn, and Ben thought the house had a spooky feeling about it. He could quite understand why no children dared venture close; it reminded him of an old house in a Halloween film that he had seen when he was younger.

Ballin waited with the horses whilst the others approached the strange cottage. Hal lifted the large metal knocker and tapped softly on the door. They waited patiently, but there was no reply. Hal knocked again, but still there was no answer.

"Hello. Is anyone home?" he shouted through the letter box.

Silence followed. Then, unexpectedly, an upstairs window opened and a scruffy-looking man peered down. He had very long, matted grey hair; a wrinkled face and a large, hooked nose. He peered down at them and dropped a folded piece of paper, before slamming the window shut without saying a word.

Hal picked up the paper and read aloud. "It says, *NOBODY WELCOME HERE. GO AWAY,*" he sighed.

Tia, Amy and Ben looked at each other in shock, and Hal knocked again. Once more the window opened and a scrunched-up piece of paper was dropped down.

Hal straightened it out before reading its contents to the others. "It says, *I'VE ALREADY TOLD YOU ONCE, NOW GO AWAY!*"

Hal again opened the letter box and shouted through. "Wimble, we haven't come here to cause you any trouble. We really need your advice. Please could you spare us just a few minutes of your time?"

Wimble didn't reply.

"We need your help, Wimble. We think you may be able to guide us to the Ancient Scrolls," Hal shouted.

All of a sudden the sound of bolts being drawn back came from the other side of the door, and it was flung open.

"Well, why didn't you say that in the first place, place, place?!" blurted Wimble as he stood before them. "You had better come in, in, in. Skipperty-skip. Hopperty-hop. In you come!"

Hal, Tia, Amy and Ben looked at each other in bewilderment as they followed the skinny, shabby-looking Wimble into the house.

"Sit yourselves down, down, down," said Wimble, pulling out the chairs from underneath the table. "Now, who wants a cup of tea, tea, tea?"

Wimble's guests looked around the untidy room. The furniture was all battered and torn. The room looked as though it hadn't been dusted in years. Dirty plates and cups were scattered everywhere, and Wimble had obviously not washed his pots in months.

"Erm, no thanks. I'm not very thirsty," Tia replied.

"Nor me!" added Amy quickly.

"I won't hear of it, it, it. Guests need a cup of tea, tea, tea. How do you like it? With mushy peas or pepper?" Wimble stared at them, waiting for a reply.

"Thank you very much for the offer, Wimble, but I really don't want a cup of tea!" Tia shuddered.

"Mushy peas it is, then," chirped Wimble, and he skipped off into the kitchen in a peculiar fashion.

"Ruby was right," whispered Tia. "He's completely insane!"

"Perhaps there is a method to his madness!" suggested Hal. "Let's just be polite and find out if he really does know anything about the Ancient Scrolls."

Wimble skipped back into the room carrying a tray containing five teacups, a teapot and a dish with a lid. "Here we are, are, are," he stammered, whilst pouring a strange purple liquid from the teapot into the cups. He then removed the lid from the dish and a mouse quickly jumped out and scurried across the table. Amy jumped backwards in alarm. The mouse leaped from the table and ran into a hole in the bottom of the living-room wall. Wimble seemed unconcerned, and scooped a spoonful of mushy peas from the dish and dropped it into one of the cups. He added peas to the other four whilst whistling a strange tune to himself. "Cheers!" he said, holding his strange concoction in the air before putting it to his lips and having a long drink. "Mmmmmm, delicious! Drink up!"

Hal held a cup to his mouth and pretended to sip the strange concoction. He glared at the others, urging them to do the same. They reluctantly put the cups to their mouths and pretended to drink. Amy heaved in disgust and quickly turned her face away from the table so Wimble wouldn't notice.

"How rude of me, I forgot the cake!" declared Wimble, jumping up from the table and rushing back into the kitchen.

"I'm fine! I'm really not very hungry!" shouted Amy, but Wimble seemed oblivious to her protests.

"Here we go, go, go," he chirped, placing a cake tin on the table. He took the cake out of the tin and sliced it up into several pieces. "Scrumptious!" he declared, popping a piece into his mouth.

As he did so, Amy noticed something wiggling in his slice of cake. She peered down at her own piece and stared in revulsion at the hundreds of maggots slithering around inside the cake. She quickly put her hand over her mouth and ran out the front door. Ben peered down at the cake and then pushed it away with his hand as Amy appeared back in the doorway, wiping her mouth.

"Now, what was it you wanted, wanted, wanted?" asked Wimble.

"We are searching for the Ancient Scrolls and were told that you may be able to help us," said Hal.

"Why me, me, me?" asked Wimble.

"We were informed that you are a very wise old man and that your knowledge of such things is tremendous," replied Hal encouragingly.

"Most people think I'm mad, mad, mad. And perhaps I am?" answered Wimble, as he pushed his matted grey hair away from his face and tucked it behind his ear.

Ben stared in amazement… surely his eyes were playing tricks on him? Wimble had two ears on the right-hand side of his head. They were large, and twitched as he talked. Ben looked at Amy in order to get her attention and then shifted his eyes to Wimble's ears. Amy gazed towards Wimble and looked at his two right ears with repulsion. She shifted her chair to see the other side of Wimble's head and tried to peer under his hair. To her horror, he also had two large, twitching ears on the left-hand side of his head!

"Well, maybe if people think you are mad, they are a little naive," added Hal, trying not to look at Wimble's ears as he spoke.

"I can tell you many things, things, things. Like, that pigs are really chickens in disguise. I tried telling some fools this once, but none of them believed me. They just said I was mad!"

Tia raised her eyebrows and looked at Hal cautiously.

"What can you tell us about the Ancient Scrolls?" asked Hal.

"The Ancient Scrolls, Scrolls, Scrolls are in Xallanpolis. People say Xallanpolis doesn't exist, but it does, does, does."

"It is said that the city of Xallanpolis was washed away by the great floods a few centuries ago. How can it still exist?" asked Hal.

"It's under the sea, of course!" declared Wimble, very matter-of-factly.

"Divers tried for many years to find Xallanpolis, but it was never found. It is said that it is just an old wives' tale and there was never such a place," said Tia.

"That's because people can't see past the end of their own noses, noses, noses!" replied Wimble. "If they tried looking a little harder they might find the obvious!"

Ben noticed Wimble's ears twitching rapidly, as he became more and more agitated.

"So how do we find this underwater city that you say still exists?" asked Hal.

"You can only find it every full moon, moon, moon. Locate the small island with a chapel. Just past the chapel you will find a rock in the sea, sea, sea. Sit there at midnight on the next full moon. Close your eyes and whisper to the night, night, night. Whisper, 'Spirits of Xallanpolis, please come to me.' Whisper it several times and your calls will be answered. The spirits will only answer children… they do not trust the adults of this world. People may have searched for Xallanpolis for many years, but nobody can find Xallanpolis… Xallanpolis must find you!"

They stared at Wimble in utter disbelief. Surely what he was saying could not be true; he must be completely insane?

Wimble looked at them, and his ears twitched uncontrollably. "Now, I have told you enough, enough, enough. Be on your way, way, way. Out you go, go, go. Be off with you now."

He stood and began ushering them out with his hands. The smell that oozed from his body was overwhelming, and again Amy had to put her hand over her mouth to prevent herself from being sick.

"Please, Wimble, you have been very helpful, but we just have a few more questions," proclaimed Hal, as he was backed up towards the entrance.

Wimble pushed them through the door in a hurry. "Not today, thank you, you, you," he chirped, as he slammed it in their faces.

The four of them stood outside in utter bewilderment.

"How did it go?" asked Ballin enthusiastically.

"Ruby was definitely right. He's as mad as a hatter!" concluded Ben.

"Maybe there could be some truth in his words?" suggested Hal unconvincingly.

"Don't be ridiculous!" added Amy. "He served us mushy peas with what he said was tea! His cake was crawling with maggots and he told us pigs are actually chickens in disguise! He's completely nuts."

"Perhaps he speaks in riddles because he wants people to think he is mad?" suggested Hal. "If we are to trust the map, he has to be the wise old man. No others live in this region. And if we don't follow his advice, where do we go from here? We are at a dead end unless we do as he advised."

"So you want us to wait for the next full moon, sit on a rock in the sea and ask the spirits of Xallanpolis to come to us? Are you mad?!" exclaimed Ben.

"Do you have any better ideas?" asked Hal.

Ben and Amy stared at Hal, wondering whether he was as insane as Wimble himself.

Chapter 12

The Ancient Scrolls

It was a clear, moonlit evening as the boat pulled into the small harbour on the island. Tonight would be the first full moon since their strange and disturbing visit to Wimble's cottage, and midnight was approaching.

"I think this is a really silly idea!" groaned Jacob, as he climbed from the boat. "Underwater cities and spirits of Xallanpolis? It just isn't going to happen. That Wimble is sending us on a wild goose chase and probably having a real good laugh whilst he's at it. We're going to feel like a right bunch of idiots sitting on a rock in the sea at midnight and whispering to spirits that don't exist!"

"It is our only hope, and stranger things have happened," declared Hal.

Ben could tell that even Hal himself was not that hopeful, but they had agreed to this at his request and Ben thought it was better just to get it over with as quickly as possible. Like the others, he thought that Wimble was completely insane and had talked absolute nonsense. However, nobody had come up with any better ideas, so it had been agreed they would at least give the absurd idea a try.

The island was in darkness; the only light was that beaming down from the bright, shining moon. The chapel stood in the shadows on the rocky headland, its silhouette looking strangely eerie against the moonlit sky. Beyond the headland they reached a tiny shingle beach and looked out across the waves and the vast ocean before them.

"Look!" Amy gasped. "There's a rock poking out of the water just over there. I wonder if that is the rock which Wimble said to call the spirits from. It's just about big enough for us all and we could probably wade out that far without getting too wet."

"I've had a good look around and it's the only rock I can see," replied Ben, trying to show a bit of enthusiasm.

"Wimble warned us that only children could find their way to the secret underwater city. I think it would be wise for us Moonbeamers to wait by the little chapel out of view," Hal said cheerfully.

"How convenient for you!" retorted Jacob sarcastically, as a look of scorn flashed across his face.

Hal ignored the comment and continued. "Remember, we will not be far and shout us if you need any help. Do you have the moonstones?"

The children checked their pockets and nodded in confirmation. The Moonbeamers wished them luck and walked off into the shadows until they were out of sight.

"I don't see why we should have to do anything those Moonbeamers tell us to do. They get to sit back and rest whilst we make complete idiots out of ourselves!"

"Oh, stop moaning, Jacob! Let's just get this over with!" said Owen.

Jacob huffed and turned away, clearly not very happy with the situation he had found himself in.

"How long have we got?" asked Amy.

"It's nearly time," Ben answered as he checked his watch. "Let's wade out to the rock and get ourselves ready."

They rolled up their trousers to above knee height and started walking out into the water. Ben gasped as the chill of the ocean struck him.

"It's freezing!" Amy shivered.

"It's so cold!" panted Owen.

"This is really a bad idea!" grunted Jacob.

The water was quite shallow and they climbed onto the rock quickly, eager to escape the coldness of the sea. The full moon shone down onto the waves and created strange shapes, bobbing up and down. An eerie silence fell over the group as they waited. Ben checked his watch and saw the hand approach midnight. He signalled to the others and they slowly started to chant.

"Spirits of Xallanpolis, please come to us… Spirits of Xallanpolis, please come to us… Spirits of Xallanpolis, please come to us…"

At first nothing happened, and Jacob looked quite pleased with himself. But then, out of nowhere, a bright moonbeam appeared and seemed to rest itself on the rock, and the water before them started to swirl. They stared at the waves in disbelief, unable to move or talk. The sea began to swirl faster, more ferociously, and three spikes started to emerge out of the water. A large, muscular man with long blond hair and a beard rose from beneath the waves. He clutched what looked like a trident, and he wore a crown of flowers around his head. The sea came up to his waist and water dripped from his bare chest.

"Why do you summon me?" he asked the children.

"Who-who-who are you?" blubbered Ben as his chest tightened with fear.

"I am Toreas, God of the Sea. Why do you summon me?"

"W-w-w-we need your help," stammered Ben.

The children stared in fear and disbelief.

"What kind of help?" asked the strange water-man.

"W-w-w-we are searching for the Ancient Scrolls!" Ben spluttered.

"I cannot bring you the Ancient Scrolls. They are in Xallanpolis and there they must remain," the man bellowed.

"We need their help!" begged Amy. "My friends here are in grave danger and only the secrets written within the Scrolls can save them."

"I can take you to the Ancient Scrolls, but I cannot bring them to you. Jump into the water and I will help you."

"B-b-but I cannot swim!" blubbered Jacob.

The others stared at him in surprise. It now made sense why Jacob had been objecting so much, but he had been too proud to admit anything.

"Do not worry yourself with that, my child, just step into the water," Toreas insisted.

Ben felt himself being drawn closer and closer to the water, as if he was in some kind of trance and unable to stop himself. He looked over to Amy and Owen and they too were slowly sliding down the rock towards the water's edge. Even Jacob had stopped protesting and was peering down. Ben slid into the water and gasped for breath. It was much deeper on this side of the rock, and the water closed over his head. For a second he panicked, but then he realised that he was floating. He looked around and saw the others in the water too. The sea around them lit up and Ben looked down into the waves. The strange water-man did not have legs, but instead a large fish-like tail. From above the waist his torso looked human, but his bottom half was that of a sea creature. Ben looked down at his own body and, to his amazement, he too no longer had any legs, but instead a large tail.

"I look like a mermaid from a story!" Amy cried.

The water no longer had the same chill and now felt satisfyingly warm.

"Come!" the merman shouted before skimming off into the deep waters.

Ben swished his tail and moved with great velocity. A smile spread across Jacob's face as he realised he could swim strongly. They followed Toreas at speed, gliding through the water like giant fish. Suddenly, the merman started to descend, and the children began to panic, afraid to put their heads beneath the water's surface. Toreas beckoned for them to follow and continued to swim down towards the seabed. The children looked at each other in fright, not knowing how long they could hold their breath under the ocean.

Ben started to swim down and the others followed reluctantly. As Ben swam deeper into the ocean he realised he could not hold his breath any longer and he made a quick gasp for air. However, to his delight, he found that he could easily breathe under the water, and he quickly spun round to face the other children.

"I can breathe!" he shouted, equally surprised by the fact that he could talk beneath the surface!

They too all gasped for air before staring at each other in disbelief. Ben, elated at his new abilities, swam enthusiastically to catch up with the merman.

The deeper they swam, the brighter the ocean became. They swam along the seabed and passed shoals of colourful fish and beautiful coral reefs. A seahorse bobbed past them and an orange clownfish glided through the water. Ben looked at his beautiful surroundings, in awe of what he was seeing. Amy pointed to the left as a school of bottle-nosed dolphins swam by, playing with their young. Ben felt that this was probably one of the most amazing and stunning sights he had ever seen.

Toreas stopped and waited for them by a large rock on the seabed. As the others caught up, he beckoned for them to follow. To their astonishment, he seemed to dive down into the rock itself and simply disappear. As the children approached the rock, they noticed that there was a small gap and realised it was an underwater cave entrance. They slowly swam into the cave, wondering where on earth it could lead, but they were not entering a dark cave, but a huge underwater city! They gasped in wonderment at the sight before them. Houses lined the streets and a palace stood majestically in the distance.

"Welcome to Xallanpolis!" Toreas announced.

The children were speechless and stared in disbelief.

"I will take you to King Bartholomew and Queen Taliana, for only they can give you permission to see the Ancient Scrolls."

They approached the palace and Toreas spoke to the guards at the grand doors. They were escorted into a large hallway where trumpet players announced their arrival. They floated down the middle of the magnificent hall towards two figures who were seated before them on large thrones.

"Your Majesties," announced Toreas, as he bowed before the King and Queen.

"Welcome, Toreas, God of the Sea," replied the King. "What brings you to us?"

"These children are from Numblebrook. I found them by the full moon, calling for us at the rock by the island. They say they are in grave danger and only the Ancient Scrolls can help them."

"Tell me, sweet children… why are you in grave danger?" asked Queen Taliana softly. "We haven't had any visitors from Numblebrook for many years. Luckily for us, people no longer think Xallanpolis exists."

"My friends are Giddles!" exclaimed Amy. "King Ados doesn't allow Giddles into Numblebrook. They entered through the Junction and now the passageway can't be found. They need to find their way home before the evil king tracks them down."

"Giddles! I haven't heard of Giddles entering the land for centuries. I wish I could help you, but the Scrolls cannot tell you how to locate the passageway; it never stays in the same place for long."

"Our only hope of finding the passage is to restore the realm to the Moonbeamers," replied Amy. "Evil King Ados has caused nothing but sadness and destruction in our land for many years. If we could find a way of locating the Orb, then the crown could be passed back to its rightful owners, the Moonbeamers, and they will be able to use their magic once again."

"Ah, I see," replied Queen Taliana. "We have kept our distance from Numblebrook for many years now as we prefer to live in peace. If I take you to see the Scrolls, it is imperative that our existence is kept secret. I understand the danger your friends are in, so I will help you if you can make me this promise."

"We will promise never to discuss this with anyone but the senior Moonbeamers," said Amy eagerly. "The Moonbeamers are loyal and kind and would never tell a soul!"

"Very well, as long as you can keep that promise, my sweet children." The Queen smiled. "Follow me!"

The Queen seemed gracious and kind. She had a pretty heart-shaped face with glittering sapphire eyes and a gentle smile. She wore her fair hair in a bun beneath her golden, jewelled crown which sparkled in the light. She led them through the palace to a small, round room at the top of one of the tall stone turrets. In the centre of the room was an enormous glass casket, and inside was a large golden-bound book. The book looked extremely old, and as Ben approached he squinted to read the title... *The Ancient Scrolls: The Secrets of Our Time.*

Queen Taliana opened a lock on the side of the casket and took out the book. She carried it over to a table at the side of the room and placed it on the wooden surface. "There you are!" she announced.

"How do we know whereabouts in the book to look?" asked Owen.

"Open it to the first page and ask the book what you want to know," replied the Queen.

The children looked at her with puzzled expressions on their faces.

"Inside are the Ancient Scrolls… it is no ordinary book. The Scrolls are full of wisdom, but this wisdom is not written in words. Open the book and you will see!" she advised.

Ben leaned over and opened the book at the first page. As he did so, a lady's face appeared within the book. She was very beautiful, with long red hair, big green eyes and a friendly smile.

"How can the Ancient Scrolls help you today?" The lady's voice rose from within the pages.

The children stared at the book in utter confusion. The Queen noticed their puzzled looks and nodded in encouragement for them to answer.

"We need help to locate the Enchanter's Orb. King Ados is an evil king and we want to restore the crown to the Moonbeamers," Ben replied in befuddled astonishment.

"That will be on page fifty-three!" the lady announced, quite matter-of-factly.

Her face sank back inside the book and the pages flipped rapidly. The children stood back and stared at the book in bewilderment. The pages settled on page fifty-three and a second lady appeared from the waist up. This lady was blonde, blue-eyed and as beautiful and friendly as the first.

"Hello. What can I help you with today?" she asked politely from within the book.

Ben repeated his question slowly and waited for her reply.

"The Enchanter's Orb is located in the keep at Cottisham Castle. To get to the keep you need to find the trapdoor which is located at the back of the throne room. This door will take you down some steps and along a passageway. At the end of the passageway you will come to some large double doors. Go through these doors, and this will lead you down to the keep. Dangerous things await anyone who tries to take the Orb; beware what lies ahead. If you should manage to succeed in this perilous task, the one who wishes to rule should place their hands on the Orb and chant the magic spell."

"Do you know what the spell is?" asked Amy hopefully.

The lady in the book cleared her throat and raised her hands as if acting in a play. She then started to chant the spell in a very expressive and powerful tone:

Oh, Orb, dear Orb, please listen to me,
Pass me your powers for all to see,
For I am the one who will rule this land well,
The power of the Sword should be mine to tell.

I will be a leader who is good and true,
Using powers wisely, which pass from you,
For I am the rightful heir of these lands,
I promise you this, as I hold out my hands.
Be loyal to me and I'll be faithful to you,
For this is my destiny, which I dearly hold true,
For I am the monarch, the monarch to be,
Your powers should pass to no one but me.

When she had finished, she lowered her hands and smiled, as if she were reverting to her true self.

The four children looked at each other in wonder.

"How do we remember all those words?" asked Ben.

"Here!" The lady smiled. A hand reached out of the book and came to within a few inches of Ben's face. In the lady's hand was an old scroll, and he took it carefully. As he unrolled it he realised it was a copy of the strange poem.

"Be careful to keep it safe," she advised. "It would not be wise to let it get into the wrong hands! Do you need me for anything else?"

"Just one more thing!" Amy asked quickly. "We are told we need a number code. Do you know of such a number?"

"That is for you to solve for yourselves, my lovelies. One of the numbers is right before your eyes! But it would not be wise for me to tell you everything!" Her eyes turned to look at Ben. "If you think hard enough, you will know how to decipher the number code. After all, this one small task will solve many of the world's problems! Now, if that is all you need me for, I must bid you farewell. Goodbye!"

The face disappeared back inside the book and the pages again started to flip over rapidly. They settled back on the first page and the red-haired lady reappeared.

"I'm glad we have been of assistance to you today! Thank you and good luck!" she said merrily, before the book slammed shut.

The children looked at each other in utter wonderment.

"This place gets weirder by the minute!" said Jacob.

Queen Taliana stepped forward from where she had been standing at the back of the room. "I think the Scrolls have decided that they have told you enough to help you on your quest. Once they close the book they do not wish to tell you any more of their secrets. Now come, I think it is about time we helped you return to Numblebrook, before the Moonbeamers begin to worry."

Queen Taliana led them back to the throne room, where they found the King and Toreas waiting.

"Were the Scrolls behaving for you today? Sometimes they can be rather rude and unhelpful!" the King laughed.

"Yes, they were rather obliging today!" giggled the Queen.

"Splendid!" roared the King.

"Thank you for your hospitality." Amy smiled. "You have been most helpful."

"I'm glad we could aid you, and I wish you all well in your quest. You should leave before nightfall; the seas can be a frightening place once the fish sleep!"

The King and Queen bade them farewell and Toreas led them back out of the city and up through the gap in the rocks into the vast ocean. They swam back over the coral reef, past many thousands of sea creatures, and then started to ascend towards the top of the water. The higher they swam, the darker it became. Eventually no fish could be seen and the sea no longer had that serene and beautiful feeling about it; it felt empty and dark.

Owen was trailing at the rear when he sensed something behind him. He turned and stared through the dark waters as a strange fear engulfed him. There was definitely something behind him, something looming in the deep currents. Then he saw it… a shark! Just as he realised what it was, it darted forwards in the water, heading straight for him. He screamed frantically, and the others turned to look behind.

"Owen!" Ben gasped.

The shark hit Owen with an almighty force. He went spinning through the water as the shark turned to make a second attempt to attack its prey before the kill. Again it darted at him and sent him hurtling through the water like a rag doll. It circled him, opening its huge jaws and flashing its many layers of razor-sharp teeth. As it was about to rush at Owen for the final time, Toreas seemed to appear from nowhere, pointing his trident at the fearful creature. He hit the shark with a tremendous blow and it angrily turned to face him. As Toreas raised his trident for a second time, the shark promptly turned and fled through the water at great speed. Owen was in a state of shock and the others swam frantically around him, checking that he had not been injured.

"Are you hurt?" Amy cried.

"I think I'm all right. Just a bit bruised and shaken," replied Owen, trembling.

"Do you think you are able to carry on swimming to the surface?" Ben asked sympathetically.

"I'll try," Owen muttered. "I just want to get out of here as quickly as possible!"

The other children swam either side of him as they continued their journey to the top of the ocean. They were all afraid after the attack and eager to get back on land as quickly as possible.

After swimming for a few more minutes, Toreas came to a stop. "This is where I will leave you!" he announced. "The top of the ocean is only fifty feet above us and you will easily be able to find your way from here."

"Please don't leave us!" cried Amy fretfully.

"You can't leave us here!" exclaimed Jacob. "We need to find the shoreline."

"My duty is now done. I have taken you to Xallanpolis and you have talked to the Ancient Scrolls. The Queen asked me to take you to the top of the ocean and I have done this. For the rest of your journey, you must continue alone."

"But what about our tails?" asked Ben. "We cannot leave the water whilst we are still part fish."

"Do not worry yourselves with that. Once you reach the air, your legs will return to normal. Now I must bid you farewell, my friends!" Toreas shouted as he sped off into the distance.

"But I can't swim with legs!" cried Jacob. "I will drown! Come back!"

Only silence followed, and the children looked at each other worriedly.

"Come on," said Ben shakily. "He's gone. We need to try and finish this journey alone. Let's go before any more sharks sense we are here!"

The children swam up to the ocean surface. Just as Toreas had advised, their tails turned back into legs as soon as they took their first breath of air. Jacob immediately started spluttering and his head dropped below the water. The others quickly swam over to help him and pulled him back to the surface.

"Get me out of here!" he screamed.

Ben looked around, desperately searching for the island, but all he could see was the vast ocean in every direction.

"I can't see any land!" cried Owen.

"He's just left us in the middle of the ocean! We're all going to drown!" sobbed Jacob as he clung to Amy.

"The moonstone… use the moonstone!" Amy shouted to Ben.

Ben felt in his pocket and quickly pulled out the stone. He held his hands above the water and started to rub the stone ferociously. As he rubbed he closed his eyes and chanted Hal's name, whilst desperately trying to tread water. The moonstone felt warm, and Ben quickly opened his eyes. It had become hazy, and he slowly saw Hal's face begin to appear.

"Ben! We have been so worried since you did not return this morning. Tia has been overwrought with anguish. We have been trying to contact you with the stone, but received no response."

"We need your help urgently! We are in the middle of the ocean! Jacob can't swim and I fear that we are all going to drown if you do not find us quickly!" cried Ben as fear clawed through him.

"Whereabouts in the ocean are you? Can you see any landmarks?" asked Hal frantically.

"No, nothing! I can't see anything but sea! I cannot tell you where we are!"

Ben could no longer keep both his hands above the ocean. As water hit the stone, Hal's face disappeared. Ben desperately tried rubbing the stone again, but to no avail.

"Where is he?" sobbed Amy. "Where has he gone?"

"I don't know!" cried Ben. "I lost contact with him and I can't get him back!"

They trod water for what seemed like a long time and took turns helping Jacob to stay afloat. Exhaustion was setting in and nobody had the energy to speak. The sea now felt cold, and they all realised that time was not on their side. Then, just as all hope was fading away, Ben noticed two dots in the sky in the distance. He gasped for breath as he tried to speak, but no words would come out. He pointed in the air and the others wearily looked towards the sky. The dots grew bigger, and as they got nearer, they slowly began to take shape.

"Shami!" Amy gasped.

A massive sense of relief swept through the children as they realised all was not lost. They frantically waved their arms in the air and shouted with all the energy they could muster. Shami and the other dragon instantly changed direction and started heading straight towards them… they had been seen! Two Moonbeamers were riding astride the dragons, and Hal leaned out into the air and shouted something down to them. Shami glided down to the ocean surface and flapped her wings wildly, spraying water in all directions. Hal and Tia helped pull the children out of the cold, vast ocean onto the safety of the dragon's backs. Ben felt weary and drained, but also ecstatic and relieved at being out of the water and astride the dragon, safe in the care of the

Moonbeamers once more. The children were given thick cloaks to wrap around their drenched and exhausted bodies. Then the dragons slowly rose into the air and headed off into the distance, leaving the vast ocean waves and Xallanpolis far behind them.

Chapter 13

The Number Code

Ben woke up to find himself lying on a large bed in a brightly lit room. The sun streamed in through the open window and Tia sat by his bed reading a book. She smiled as he opened his eyes.

"Where am I?" he asked.

"We're at Ruby's inn; we didn't want to risk going back to the Citadel. The King knows you are with the Moonbeamers because of the magic Hal used to destroy the red dragon. You were very weary when we pulled you from the sea. You have slept for two days and we've been very worried!"

"The magic spell!" Ben exclaimed fraughtly. "The lady inside the book gave me the magic spell… where is it? I didn't lose it in the sea, did I?"

"Do not worry yourself, Ben, the spell is safe. We found it rolled up in your pocket; it was very wet but we could still just about read the words. Amy awoke yesterday and told us all about your journey to Xallanpolis. She told us about the Ancient Scrolls and the ladies in the book. It was very fulfilling to hear that Xallanpolis really does exist and that your journey was worthwhile."

"How are Jacob and Owen?" asked Ben. "Jacob didn't tell us that he couldn't swim!"

"They are both fine, although I think Jacob is a little embarrassed at not being honest with you all!" she laughed.

There was a knock at the door and Hal and Amy entered the room. Amy looked relieved that Ben was awake and smiled at him fondly.

"Ah, Ben, young man, you have woken up at last! That was a very long sleep you had. How are you feeling?" Hal asked.

"I feel fine, although I'm a little hungry."

"I'll have Ruby arrange for some soup to be brought up, and then if you feel up to it we can all meet to discuss the next part of our journey. I have to commend you for your successful journey to Xallanpolis and for retrieving the hidden spell. You are a very brave boy. This is the closest we have been to finding the Orb for many years, and without your help we would not be here. Hopefully, soon, we will be able to repay you by finding the passage so that you can return home. This you truly deserve. All we need to do now is solve the number code, but we are very confused! We were hoping that maybe you could help with this too. The inn is closed until later today, so we will meet downstairs and discuss what our next plan will be!"

After Ben had eaten, the group gathered in the bar downstairs. Ruby fetched drinks as Hal spread sheets of paper across the table.

"We have followed each verse of the riddle, which means two things. Firstly, we should have all the numbers to solve the number code, and secondly, we need to find a way into the keep to retrieve the Orb. I can think of a reasonable solution to the second problem, but I am struggling with this code!" Hal confessed.

"What, you mean you know a way into the keep without being seen?" asked Amy in surprise.

"Not into the keep itself, but I do know a secret way into the castle!" Hal replied. "When my great-great-great-grandfather, King Semba, ruled these lands, he decided to have a secret tunnel dug. He was afraid that if the castle ever came under attack, his family would be trapped. Very few people ever knew about the tunnel and only a handful of Moonbeamers know of it today. A long time ago, when my father was king and I was but a wee child, he showed me the tunnel and told me that it must be kept a secret.

The tunnel runs from the castle to a small church in the woods. The Moonbeamers occasionally used the church and the priest made sure that the secret of the tunnel stayed well hidden. Since the crown was stolen from the Moonbeamers, the church has not been in use and is locked to passers-by. As far as we are aware, the passage has never been discovered by King Ados and his family. The entrance in the castle is hidden well and would not be found easily. I have a friend who resides in the wood near to the church; the Unicerons think that he is just a recluse, but he acts as our lookout. As far as we know, the King and his men have never taken any particular interest in the church or been seen there. If the King had discovered the tunnel, I'm sure that he would have his men patrolling the area."

"Fantastic!" replied Amy. "What do we do once we are inside the castle? The lady in the book said that there is a trapdoor at the back of the throne room. Is the tunnel near this room?"

"Not exactly!" Hal answered. "Once we are inside the castle, we need to be careful that we are not seen. It would be best to enter the castle at night as most people will be sleeping. Most of the night guards on duty will be guarding the castle wall and gates. Hopefully, only a handful will be patrolling the inside of the building."

"That's one problem solved, then!" added Ballin. "Now we just have to decipher the number code!"

"Let's look back at the riddle and write down the numbers we have, then we can try and piece together what links them," suggested Hal, not looking altogether confident. Ben thought that he had probably been racking his brains trying to decipher the numbers since they had arrived back at the inn two days ago.

"The first verse that relates to a number is the verse about the well," advised Ballin, before reading it aloud:

Deep in the eucalyptus wood
Lies the Gothic Well.
How many steps
To ring the golden bell?

"We counted 162!" exclaimed Ben. "All three of us counted the same number, so we can't all be wrong!"

The others nodded and Hal wrote the number down before reading out the next verse:

Hidden in the caves
Is the red dragon's lair.
Count the spikes on his back;
Beware of the bear.

"The dragon had nineteen spikes!" said Owen. "I counted them several times so I know I definitely didn't make any mistakes."

"Me too," Ben agreed. "I also counted nineteen."

"How many did you count, Jacob?" said Owen in a sarcastic tone, still annoyed that Jacob had left Ben and himself alone to enter the dragon's lair. Jacob turned away without replying and Hal quickly read on:

Down in the glen
Dwells the wise old man.
How can he hear you?
LISTEN to his wisdom if you can.

Deep in the sea
Rest the Ancient Scrolls.
Be sure to read them carefully;
Beware the deadly souls.

"Neither of these verses mentions a number. I'm sure we must have missed something here!" said Hal as he looked at the others for suggestions.

"No, wait!" Ben exclaimed. "Amy asked the lady in the book what she knew about the number code, and she told us that one of the numbers was right before our eyes!"

"The only number which was right before our eyes was the page number," Owen said. "From what I can remember she was on page fifty-three of the book!"

"Brilliant, Owen, I never thought of that!" Ben answered in delight.

Hal looked pleased as he wrote down the number and then continued with the riddle.

The riddle reveals the spell,
But the numbers are all mixed up high.
Only one chance to get them right;
They are all 'pie in the sky'.

"So we need to work out how to rearrange the numbers to make a code!" suggested Ballin.

With puzzled expressions, they looked at the numbers which Hal had written down:

"The verse must be a clue to deciphering the code," added Hal, "but I just cannot work out how!"

"The riddle says the numbers are *all 'pie in the sky'*," said Tia. "Is this some kind of clue?"

"As Ben said when we first looked at the riddle in detail, 'pie in the sky' could have several meanings."

Ben jumped up from his seat. "I think I've got it!" he declared. "Pass me the pen, quickly!" Hal handed him the pen and he began frantically scribbling numbers on the paper.

"What is it?" Tia asked. "What do these numbers mean?"

"I think the line *'pie in the sky'* might be a trick," Ben answered excitedly. "When I entered this land through Labyrinth Junction, I noticed mathematical formulae written on the wall in the cavern. One of the numbers was pi! Pi is the ratio of a circle's circumference to its diameter! My older brother learnt it for his homework, so I tried memorising the numbers myself as a challenge!" He looked at the numbers he had scribbled down.

"Pi is 3.1415926. The old witch at the Junction told me that mathematics solves lots of the world's problems, but many people are just too ignorant to see it. She said that I would learn that one day. Perhaps this is what she meant!"

"Oh, I do hope you're right!" Amy added excitedly. "Remember what the lady in the book said to you, too! She said, '…this one small task will solve many of the world's problems!' Perhaps she was referring to what the witch had already hinted at."

Ben looked at the numbers that he had jotted down. He started crossing off those which Hal had already written, to see if they matched his own. His face fell.

"I have the number four missing! It doesn't make sense!" he cried in despair.

"Let's look back at the verse with no number," suggested Ballin. "It has to be in there somewhere as we have solved all the other verses."

Down in the glen
Dwells the wise old man.
How can he hear you?
LISTEN to his wisdom if you can.

Everyone studied the riddle in silence with confused looks on their faces, when suddenly Amy stood up in excitement.

"Wait, I think I know why!" she exclaimed. "It says, *LISTEN to his wisdom.* '*LISTEN*' is in capital letters; surely this is the clue! You listen with your ears, and Wimble had four ears. This must be the number four we are looking for?"

A wide grin appeared across Hal's face. "By golly, you two… I think you have just solved the riddle!" he laughed, as he fondly patted them both on the back.

"So, now we have the code and we also have the magic spell!" exclaimed Ballin enthusiastically. "Now all that's left is to go in search of the Enchanter's Orb!"

Happiness flowed through the room as the group realised their adventures were nearer to being fulfilled.

Chapter 14

The Enchanter's Orb

After two days of preparations the group set off on their journey to the old church in the woods. They travelled by horseback and tried to ride via covered routes so that they would not be seen. Sometimes they rode under the cover of darkness. In daylight they travelled through thick forest, or rested in villages where they knew residents that could be trusted.

On the fourth day, they arrived at the cottage of Nalark, the priest who had once presided over the church. The community of Moonbeamers were regular churchgoers until they had been banished to the Citadel by King Ados. Nalark was now an old man and the church had had its doors locked to the public for many years, but he still held the keys to the building and checked on it from time to time. He was an old friend of the Moonbeamers and had known about the passage for decades, keeping it secret from all he knew.

Hal knocked at the cottage door. It was answered by a small, chubby man with white hair and a beard.

"Hal! Good gracious! I haven't seen you in these parts for a long time!" Nalark chirped, as he gave Hal a friendly hug. "And Tia… oh, this is a lovely surprise… come in, come in."

They entered the cottage and were led to a lovely sitting room with large, comfy sofas, and a blazing fire burning in the hearth. Ben immediately felt at ease and welcome here, and was glad for the rest. Nalark brought hot drinks and biscuits and the children took them gratefully.

"So what brings you here?" Nalark asked, after everyone had been introduced.

"We have come to ask for your help," replied Hal. "We know where the Enchanter's Orb is located, and we are going to try and take back what is rightfully ours. King Ados has ruled this land unfairly for far too long and we want to restore peace and happiness to Numblebrook. We intend to enter the castle via the secret tunnel, and this is where we need your help."

"If it means overthrowing King Ados, I will gladly give you all the help I can. I am getting very old now and I would like to see peace restored to these lands before my time is up. It would mean the world to me to see people coming through the doors of my church again."

"We need you to unlock the church and help us open up the entrance to the tunnel. Shadrack will take the horses to a nearby village. Once we have entered the passage, we need you to keep watch over the church. Act as though nothing is out of the ordinary. Hopefully, when we return, the realm will once again belong to the Moonbeamers and King Ados will reign no more!"

Nalark smiled and nodded enthusiastically.

A few hours later they assembled in a small, circular room at the back of the church. The room was empty except for a large wooden bookcase and table.

"The entrance to the tunnel has not been opened up for many years," said Nalark. "I wish you luck, my friends, and hope that when I see you again, the crown will be yours."

He walked over to the bookcase, removed a book and pressed something in the gap where the book had been. Ben and Amy stared in amazement as the bookcase swung outwards to reveal a dark underground tunnel.

"These should light the way," said Hal, as he handed lanterns to each one of the group. They slowly entered the tunnel and squinted as their eyes adjusted to the darkness.

After bidding them farewell, Nalark pushed the bookcase back into its original position. It made a grating sound and the light in the tunnel quickly dimmed. Ben turned to look behind him, realising that the opening and the bookcase could no longer be seen.

"Come on," said Hal. "Let's get going."

Steep steps wound downwards in front of them. The tunnel was quite rocky underfoot and occasionally Ben almost lost his footing. Water dripped in places and the passage was cold, damp and dark. Sometimes the tunnel would open up into small dome-shaped spaces, where there were ledges which could be used as seating. Ben was beginning to feel a little claustrophobic and couldn't wait to see daylight again. Occasionally, a bat would fly along the passageway and startle him, and he wondered how these creatures could find their way to such a place.

After walking for several hours, they eventually came to a dead end and Ben wondered whether this could be the furthermost point of the tunnel.

"This is where the passage ends," Hal announced. "It is the early hours of the morning, so hopefully most people in the castle will be sleeping. When I press this button, the wall will open up and we will find ourselves in the castle library. Like in the church, the tunnel is hidden behind a bookcase. Hopefully, nobody will be in the library at this hour and we can enter the castle unseen, but we still need to be extremely careful. From there we need to make our way to the throne room and find the trapdoor. Ben, Owen and Jacob, it is probably wise for you to eat the three remaining sweets before we enter. If anyone should see us, at least you will be invisible. Is everyone ready?"

They all nodded, so Ben handed Owen and Jacob a red sweet each. They took them gratefully, happy to know that they would not be seen by any prying eyes. Once they were invisible, Hal asked them to stand well back and then proceeded to feel the crevices in the wall. Eventually, after what seemed like several minutes, he found what he had been searching for. With a little pull, the wall swung outwards and the tunnel opened up to reveal a huge circular library. They waited for a few seconds and listened for voices. Nothing could be heard, so they crept out into the castle.

They sneaked out of the library and along a hallway which led towards the throne room. As Ben was invisible, he went ahead and checked open doorways and corners for any guards who might be on duty. A couple of times they heard voices coming towards them and hid in dark rooms until the guards had passed.

Eventually, they came to a huge hall with two grand thrones at one end. Owen kept a lookout in the hallway whilst the others searched for the trapdoor. Ballin moved a large rug which was on the floor and the trapdoor was found. They quickly opened it and found a long flight of steps going down. Hal whispered for Owen to join them and they all climbed through the trapdoor and crept down the steps. Ballin and Josiah tried to pull the rug as far back over the trapdoor as they could, before closing it and joining the others.

"We need to reach the Orb quickly, before someone notices that the rug has been moved," Ballin advised.

They hurried along the passage in silence and came to some hefty wooden doors at the far end.

"The lady in the book said that these doors lead directly down into the keep!" whispered Amy.

"She also said that dangerous things await us there!" Jacob shuddered.

"We have come this far; we need to complete our task!" replied Hal. "There are eight of us here and three of you are invisible. We have weapons and we know the number code and the magic spell. If we tackle this together I'm convinced we can do this. Now let's go and retrieve what rightfully belongs to the Moonbeamers!"

They opened the double wooden doors and a wide flight of steps descended in front of them. At the bottom was an enormous room. It was brightly lit by blazing fires, each burning in the saucer-shaped top of a tall pillar. As they climbed down the steps the heat from the flames was so intense that the Giddles began to feel their bodies tingle.

"The heat… it's making me visible again!" yelled Jacob.

"And me!" Owen shrieked.

"Do not worry yourselves, boys," said Hal. "We are all here to help protect each other."

They reached the bottom of the steps and started to make their way through the shimmering heat across the large stone room. Suddenly they heard a strange hissing sound and stopped to listen.

"What is that?" Jacob trembled.

"I don't know… let's keep moving!" Ballin whispered.

Apprehensively, they slowly crept forward, searching the room with their eyes as they went. The noise started to get louder, and Ben shuddered at the prospect of what they were about to encounter.

Tia spotted something moving to her right and leapt sideways towards the others. "Over there!" she screeched.

They looked in horror as a gigantic, green, six-legged creature crept out from behind one of the pillars. It turned its ugly head to look directly at them with its bulging eyes. It had two wings and two large antennae, and its two front legs looked like huge, bent, spiky arms. The hissing sound was coming from the grotesque creature, as it rubbed its wings against its huge abdomen.

"It's a giant praying mantis!" screamed Ben.

The mantis started walking towards them, turning its head with each step, the spikes on its legs twitching as it went. They stood glued to the spot and raised their swords in defence. The creature leapt at them, grabbing Jacob with its two front legs and thrusting him upwards towards its massive jaws. With swords drawn, Hal, Ballin and Josiah quickly returned the attack. With one mighty blow, Hal struck the monster, severing one of its long back legs. The insect screeched in pain as Jacob dropped to the floor. It made a strange hissing sound and instantly started to shake. They looked in horror as the beast's skin began to peel and fall to the floor.

"It's dead… we've killed it!" cried Amy shedding joyful tears. But her glee was short-lived as she watched the mantis step outside its skin and hobble towards them.

"It's moulting! It's called its exoskeleton. It's not dead! Stand back… praying mantises grow when they've shed their exoskeleton," sobbed Tia in despair.

As the creature moved towards them, it started to grow in size, and soon its head was almost touching the high ceiling. Amy screamed, and Jacob ran back towards the rear of the hall, still shaking with fear from his ordeal. The gigantic insect jumped at its prey and this time caught Josiah with its spiky arms, lifting him into the air and flinging him across the stone room. The others hacked frantically at the mantis, severing more limbs, but still the beast hobbled towards them, flapping its wings and hissing.

"We can't kill it!" screamed Amy. "It won't die!"

"Use some magic!" yelled Jacob in desperation from the far side of the room.

"If I use magic now, the King will know we are here before we even make it to the Orb. We have to try and kill it ourselves!" exclaimed Hal frantically.

The insect leapt at them again, flapping its wings ferociously. It grabbed Tia with its mighty front legs and lifted her high into the air. The others tried to swing their swords towards the mantis' body, but were flung backwards by the fast flapping of the creature's huge wings. Hal ran behind it and began to climb one of the burning pillars, finding footholds on the rough stone surface. As he neared the top, he jumped and landed on the creature's back. The mantis started to leap and screech in anger, attempting to throw Hal from its body. He held on for dear life and slowly tried to pull himself up towards the beast's neck. The mantis held Tia with its spiky legs, whilst spinning in fury. Its head spun round and its bulging eyes stared angrily at Hal, but as the creature opened its jaws, he lifted his sword and plunged it into the insect's body. For a second the mantis stood still, staring at Hal in fury as Tia fell to the floor. Then, in an instant, its massive body crashed to the ground.

"You've done it, Hal… you've killed it!" yelled Ben.

Hal was exhausted but smiling. Amy ran to Tia to check that she was not injured, and they hugged each other and wiped away exultant tears.

"We need to keep moving!" said Hal. "I'm hoping the King has not heard the commotion, but I fear that this may not be the case."

Although elated that they had killed the giant praying mantis, they knew that more danger lay ahead and that they needed to move quickly.

They continued through the chamber, looking frantically for anything that could lead them to the Orb. There was a large, empty alcove at the far end, but at first sight it revealed nothing, and they looked at each other in despair.

"There must be something here!" said Ben. "The lady in the book would not lie! It has to be somewhere down here."

"Keep searching," said Hal. "Look for anything that could give us a clue."

They scanned the room desperately, looking in every corner and crevice.

Suddenly Tia alerted the others, pointing to what looked like a square piece of stone sticking out of the alcove wall.

Hal ran over to her and examined it in detail. "It looks like a button," he said. "Perhaps it will reveal a secret room or somehow lead us to the Orb!"

The others joined him, while Amy continued to look over at the far side of the room for anything that could give them a clue.

"Perhaps this back wall in the alcove is false and the button will reveal what is behind it?" suggested

Ballin hopefully, tapping on the panel. "It sounds as though it could be hollow. I think we should press the button and see what happens."

Hal knocked on the wall. "I think you could be right, Ballin. I don't think we have any other option but to try. There's no way out of this room. Let's press it and see what happens." He placed his hand on the stone and gently pushed it. They all smiled when they saw it slowly move backwards into the stone.

"I told you it was a button!" Ballin grinned, feeling extremely pleased with himself.

They waited for the secret to be uncovered. But to their horror, a panel of metal bars like a cage door slid from the ceiling above them and trapped them in the alcove.

"It was a trick!" declared Ben. "How do we get out?"

Amy came running over. "What's happened? What's happened?" she screamed, as she peered at her friends caged in the alcove.

"We pressed a piece of rock that looked like a button. We thought it might reveal a secret room. Look around on the walls outside, there might be another button that makes the cage door go back up!" cried Tia.

As Amy scanned the walls outside the alcove, the others tried lifting the metal panel, but it was stuck to the floor and would not budge.

"I've found something!" shouted Amy. "I think this could be it… it's a square piece of stone sticking out of the wall."

"Press it quickly!" replied Hal. "Get us out of here!"

Amy pressed the rock, and nothing happened for a few seconds. Then, to everyone's horror, metal spikes protruded from the ceiling of the alcove. They extended for about a foot and then stopped. The captives looked up in horror at the spikes and wondered what was about to happen. Then an alarm sounded… some kind of warning siren. The floor in the alcove began to move! It was moving upwards, moving them towards the spikes. Tia screamed, and Jacob started banging on the metal bars.

"We're going to die… we're going to die!" he howled.

Amy looked at her friends, not knowing how she could help.

"Amy, look around for another button!" screamed Hal. "There must be another button!"

Amy was shaking with fear as she frantically searched around. The alcove floor moved higher and higher with each second that passed.

"Lie flat on the floor!" Josiah shouted to the others in the alcove. Everyone immediately obeyed, lying as flat as possible as the floor rose upwards towards the spikes.

"I've found three more buttons all next to each other!" shouted Amy in desperation. "I don't know which one to press!"

"Just press any!" shouted Hal. The spikes were now only a few feet above them, and Hal looked at his friends panic-ridden faces. Amy quickly pressed the first rock button and the floor immediately stopped moving. Relief appeared on the faces of those trapped in the alcove, and they waited, hoping that the floor would move back downwards or the spikes would ascend back into the ceiling, but nothing happened.

"Amy, press another button!" shouted Hal from inside the alcove.

"What if I press the wrong one?!" Amy sobbed.

"We have no other option, Amy! You need to press one!"

Amy held out her hand, not knowing which button to press. Fearing the worst, she placed the palm of her hand over the second button, closed her eyes and pressed it, not daring to look at her friends. The floor started to move upwards again, and she heard Tia's screams. She quickly put her hand to the final button and pressed with all her might. She watched as, immediately, the floor again came to a standstill. After a few seconds a siren sounded, the floor started to move downwards again and the spikes disappeared into the ceiling.

Her friends sat up and hugged each other as Amy collapsed to the floor and sobbed in exultation. As the floor hit ground level, another alarm sounded and the metal bars rose to the ceiling, freeing the trapped friends. Then, as the relieved, shaking group stepped clear of the alcove, they heard another strange sound and looked behind them. To their astonishment, the far wall of the alcove was opening out to reveal a secret room behind it!

"I knew it… I knew it!" cried Ballin excitedly.

They slowly walked through the open alcove and into the room beyond. Before them was a large area of sand with several rows of stepping stones stretching to the far side of the keep. Beyond the sand they could see a large circle of stones with a glass dome on top. Floating inside the dome was the Orb, the Orb they had been searching for, glowing and shimmering and rotating in the air!

"The Orb!" gasped Amy. The friends smiled at each other, knowing that it was now within their reach.

"The Orb is yours for the taking, Hal." Tia smiled. "You should go and take what is rightfully yours!"

"We need to use the number code and magic spell first," replied Hal enthusiastically.

"You will probably need to use the code to release the glass," suggested Ballin.

"Well, let's go and have a look!" said Hal, smiling, as he began to walk across the stepping stones towards the Orb. Ballin followed closely behind.

Suddenly, Hal lost his balance and realised that the stones were sinking into the sand. He felt himself being sucked down and tried to move his feet, but they were stuck fast, and the more he tried to free himself, the lower he sank. "Help me… it's quicksand!" he yelled.

Ballin gasped and held out his hand to help his friend, but to his horror, he also began to submerge into the sand.

"Keep still!" shouted Hal. "The more you struggle, the further you sink!"

The sand was now up to their waists. They tried to keep as still as possible, afraid that they would disappear completely beneath the surface.

"Don't stand on the stones!" Ballin shouted to the others.

Something came into Ben's mind and he counted the number of rows of stepping stones. "What if we don't need to use the number code for the Orb?" he blurted. "What if we have to use the code when crossing the stepping stones?"

"I don't understand!" Tia panicked as she watched her friends sinking further into the quicksand.

"There are eight numbers in the code, and there are also eight rows of stepping stones!" answered Ben. The number code is 3.1415926. What if we were to step out three stones on the left-hand row, then step to the right to the second row? The next number is one, so step forward one more stone and then across to the third row. The next number is four, so move forward four more stones and then step to the right again. Continue to move in this pattern until we reach the far side. It might work! Then if we know which stones won't sink, we can work out how to help Hal and Ballin!"

"The only way to find out is to try it!" shouted Hal fearfully. "But be careful!"

"I'll do it!" replied Ben. "I could be wrong and I don't want anyone else to come to any harm over my mistake."

"Be careful, Ben!" whispered Amy.

Ben moved in front of the first row of stones. He began stepping out, counting the stones as he crossed. "One, two, three." He stood still on the third stepping stone and paused, afraid to make his next move. The stones stayed firmly on top of the sand and did not move. He carefully stepped across to the next row and held his breath. The stone held fast.

"The next number is one, Ben," shouted Owen in encouragement.

Ben stepped forward one more stone, then across to the next row. Again the stones remained rigid and did not submerge into the sand.

"Now four, Ben," yelled Amy.

Ben's heart was in his throat as he moved forward another four steps, and again stepped across to the next row. With the shouts of encouragement from his friends he continued the pattern: forward one and across, forward five and across, forward nine and across, forward two and across. His heart pounded as he moved forward on the final six stones and found himself standing on the far side of the sand in front of the glowing Orb. He released a huge exhalation of pent-up breath as he heard the others clapping in excitement.

"Now we know which stones to stand on, we need to help Hal and Ballin quickly," shouted Ben. "There is a long pole hooked onto the wall over here. I presume this is to help people out!" He ran over, unhooked the pole and turned back towards the sand.

"I don't think that will be necessary!" boomed a voice from back inside the alcove.

The friends turned around, and to their horror saw King Ados and his guards standing in the entrance to the room. Amy, Jacob and Owen were pushed to the ground by the Unicerons and their hands were tied behind their backs. Tia and Josiah were shoved against the rocky wall, tied together and gagged. Ben stared in disbelief and shock from the other side of the sand, feeling helpless and afraid.

"So, Haligan Lexin… you thought that you could trick me, did you? You thought that you could steal my Orb and become king. You didn't think I would make it that easy for you, did you? And you used Giddles to help you! Well, here you are stuck in quicksand. What are you going to do now? You can't reach the Orb whilst you are cemented in there, can you?" King Ados broke into a callous and wicked laugh and pointed the glowing Sword of Gwyntog at Hal. "Shall I finish you off or enjoy watching you slowly sink?" A sardonic smile gleamed in his eyes.

"You might stop me from becoming king," bellowed Hal in retaliation, "but there are others who could make a worthy king." He turned his head towards Ben. "Ben, get the Orb! The throne is yours to take! You are the one who brought us this riddle and helped us solve it. You are the worthy king of this land… go and take what is rightfully yours!"

"But it is *not* mine to take," shouted Ben in bewilderment. "The Moonbeamers are the true kings of this land."

"No, Ben, the old witch led you to us. You are the true king. Take the Orb, Ben, before it is too late!" yelled Hal in desperation.

King Ados glared at Hal in disbelief and then turned to stare at Ben. Ben knew he had to do everything he could to free the land of this evil king. He began to run towards the Orb.

"Seize him!" roared the King as rage swept over him.

The King's men started to run across the stepping stones, slipping and sinking into the sand.

"You imbeciles! Do I have to do everything myself?!" The King's blood boiled as he quickly jumped onto the first row of stones and started to count out the number sequence in order to reach the far side.

"Run!" Amy shouted to Ben.

Ben reached the Orb and touched the glass protecting it. The dome opened up and he placed his hands on the Orb's glowing surface. It felt warm to touch, and a haze of glittering light lit up his hands and spread a quiver of goosebumps through his entire body. He felt a burst of energy enter him and engulf his inner self. As he began to chant the

magic spell, he instantly felt a renewed confidence and strength:

Oh, Orb, dear Orb, please listen to me,
Pass me your powers for all to see,
For I am the one who will rule this land well,
The power of the Sword should be mine to tell.

As he chanted the spell, flashes of light escaped from the Orb, shooting around his head. He tried to concentrate on the spell, but felt the speeding wisps of light trying to pull him away.

"Ignore them, Ben, ignore them. They are the deathly souls the riddle warns us about. They will try and stop you from taking the Orb, but they cannot hurt you. Ignore them!" Hal shouted.

Ben kept his eyes tightly closed, trying to block out all evil, and continued to recite:

I will be a leader who is good and true,
Using powers wisely, which pass from you,
For I am the rightful heir of these lands,
I promise you this, as I hold out my hands.

Out of nowhere, Ben heard a familiar voice whispering his name. He glanced over into the corner of the keep and, to his disbelief, saw his mother standing there. She was beckoning him to come to her. He paused for a moment and smiled.

"Don't listen to her, Ben! It's not your mother, it's the deathly souls trying to play tricks with your mind. Ignore her; I promise you it's not your mother!" Hal shrieked, hoping and praying that he could convince Ben to listen to him.

Ben had not seen his mother for weeks and felt drawn to the image of her in the corner. He desperately wanted to feel her arms around him again, and to tell her how sorry he was for the worry he had caused, but slowly he tried to take heed of Hal's warning. He regained his composure and turned back to look at the Orb and realised it was becoming very hot in his hands. He glanced behind him and saw that King Ados had reached the far side of the stepping stones and was running towards him, brandishing the Sword of Gwyntog. With renewed determination, Ben's concentration returned to the Orb and he continued to chant the spell.

Be loyal to me and I will be faithful to you,
For this is my destiny, which I dearly hold true,
For I am the monarch, the monarch to be,
Your powers should pass to no one but me.

As he finished chanting the spell, he saw King Ados swinging the Sword towards him. Ben's blood ran cold and he held his breath in fear, anticipating the impact, but none came and the glowing Sword suddenly dimmed and dropped from King Ados' hand. The King hollered in fury and went to pick it up. As he did so, it scalded his hand and he dropped it again, screaming in pain.

"No!" he shouted in absolute rage. Fury blinded him and he sank to the floor in anger and disbelief.

Ben, still holding the Orb in one hand, bent down to pick up the magical Sword of Gwyntog. As he touched it, it began to glow and shimmer radiantly. He held it high in the air. Ben felt an enormous rush of power from the Sword, and knew, in that moment, that the Sword now served no one but him.

Chapter 15

Crowning of a King

News spread fast and the inhabitants of the land of Numblebrook were overjoyed. King Ados ruled no more and at last the people could look forward to a new future. The name on everyone's lips was that of Benjamin Giddle, a young earthling boy who had saved the land from evil and destruction. Today was to be his coronation day, and people had come from far and wide to catch sight of their future king.

King Ados had been banished to Numblebrook Island Prison to meet the same fate he had sentenced many others to. Innocent prisoners had been freed and talked of owing their lives to the brave earthling child, a national hero. The Unicerons no longer served the evil King Ados and now served the one with the power of the Sword… Benjamin Giddle.

"How are you feeling, Ben… are you a little nervous?" asked Hal. He looked out of one of the high windows at Cottisham Castle as eager crowds were gathering outside. "Many people have come to see you crowned king. You have made them very happy, Benjamin."

"I do not feel that I am a worthy king," replied Ben. "I am grateful to the Moonbeamers and all these people who gather outside, but I am just a young child from Earthlingcragg. I don't have the wisdom needed to be a king."

"Do not worry yourself, Ben. I am your right-hand man and will teach you everything I know. Don't forget, I owe my life to you!"

Ben smiled at Hal, but inside he felt a sense of emptiness and missed his family.

There was a soft tap on the door and Amy and Tia walked into the room. Both looked exceptionally beautiful in their long, flowing gowns and sparkling tiaras.

"Are you both ready? The ceremony is about to start and people are waiting," Tia advised fondly.

Ben gave a deep sigh and nodded. Amy placed her hand on his arm and gave him a reassuring pat.

As they stepped through the doorway and into the castle grounds, they were greeted by the cheers of thousands of people. Trumpets played as Ben walked through the crowds wearing his majestic robes. Unicerons lined the walkway and bowed as Ben passed. Hal, Tia and Amy followed close behind him.

A stage had been erected in the middle of the large courtyard and the throne awaited him. He walked up the steps and saw Jacob and Owen sitting over to one side of the congregation. Ballin, Josiah and Shadrack sat at the front and cheered Ben as he climbed the steps.

Nalark stood in the centre of the stage dressed in long white robes. "Welcome, Benjamin Giddle, future King of Numblebrook! Please kneel," he stated.

Ben knelt on the soft cushion before him, but a weight settled in his heart and he was unsure that this was what he wanted. He felt proud of what he had achieved and elated that Numblebrook was free of its evil king. But sorrow shredded his insides, for he ached to see his family again and his body felt laden with sadness.

"Will you solemnly promise to serve the people of Numblebrook, to use the Orb and the Sword of Gwyntog for the good of the land, and to be a loyal and trusted king for your people?" Nalark asked.

Ben remained silent, trapped in his own thoughts, and the crowd began to stir, waiting for his response.

"You need to say you solemnly promise!" whispered Amy nervously, wondering why he was not responding.

Ben slowly rose to his feet and then turned to address the crowd. "I am sorry, but I cannot solemnly swear to serve the people of Numblebrook. I am truly honoured that so many people have travelled from far and wide to see me crowned king, but I am not the one who should rightfully rule this land. I helped overthrow the evil King Ados and I hold the power of the Enchanter's Orb and the Sword of Gwyntog, but the crown should not have been mine for the taking. The true kings of this land are the Moonbeamers. It is they who had the crown stolen from them. They ruled this land well for many years, with loyalty, love, kindness and respect. It is they who can restore happiness to this land, not I. I do not have the experience and loyalty that I need to rule this beautiful place. I am proud to have been part of solving the riddle and bringing peace to Numblebrook, but although I love and admire this special land and the friends I have made here, my loyalties lie elsewhere. I would not make a good king when my heart lies in my homeland."

Gasps could be heard from the crowd.

"Without you, Benjamin Giddle, we would not have been able to solve the riddle and win back the Orb. You have come to this land and brought peace. The Orb and the realm *are* rightfully yours," Hal announced.

"No, Hal, you are the rightful king. The Orb was stolen from your father and you were next in line to rule. You were raised as royalty and I cannot take that from you." Ben walked over to the glass cabinet where the Orb glowed in all its glory. He took it in his hands and carried it over to where Hal was standing.

"I want you to take the Orb and chant the magic spell. I want the power of the Orb to pass to you, and I want the Sword of Gwyntog to become yours. You are the rightful king, Haligan Lexin, not I."

The crowd roared in approval and started shouting Hal's name. Hal placed his hands on the Orb and looked at Ben.

"Are you sure you want to do this, Ben?" he whispered.

"I've never been so sure of anything in my life!" Ben answered happily.

Hal turned to the crowd and began to chant the magic spell.

Oh, Orb, dear Orb, please listen to me,
Pass me your powers for all to see,
For I am the one who will rule this land well,
The power of the Sword should be mine to tell.
I will be a leader who is good and true,
Using powers wisely, which pass from you,
For I am the rightful heir of these lands,
I promise you this as I hold out my hands.
Be loyal to me and I will be faithful to you,
For this is my destiny, which I dearly hold true,
For I am the monarch, the monarch to be,
Your powers should pass to no one but me.

As Hal spoke the words, the Orb began to shimmer and dazzle in his hands. He felt the power of the Orb

flowing through his veins and the crowds cheered in encouragement. The Sword dimmed in Ben's hands and he felt the energy vanish from it. As he passed it to Hal, a smile appeared on Hal's face. Lights engulfed the Sword as its magic returned, and cheers could be heard throughout the castle grounds. Hal held the Sword high in the air and it glimmered in all its glory.

Ben smiled at the wondrous sight before his eyes, knowing that he had made the right decision. He had fulfilled his duty, and now he was ready to go home.

Chapter 16

Home Sweet Home

The day after Hal was crowned king and the celebrations were over, he stood with Ben on the hillside, looking down at the ravine and the floating islands in the distance. Jacob and Owen sat on the grass with Amy, Tia and the other senior Moonbeamers, all deep in thought. Nobody spoke, and only the whisper of the breeze and the sound of Shami munching on the green grass could be heard.

Ben gave a deep sigh and turned towards Jacob and Owen. "I think the time is right… are you ready?"

"As ready as we will ever be," chirped Owen.

"Are you sure you can do this, Hal?" asked Jacob.

"With the Sword in my possession, I now have

use of all the old magic, so there is no reason why this should not work," he answered. "If everyone stands back, I will see if I can summon the passage to us!"

Ben, Owen and Jacob held their breath, praying that this would work and they would see their families once again. Hal held his Sword in the air. He closed his eyes and started to mutter words which the Giddles could not understand. His voice rose and his face reddened with the effort. The Sword glowed in his hand and light shot out from its blade. Shami stopped munching grass and stared warily at Hal, wondering what this strange phenomenon could be. Hal continued to roar foreign words and the blade brightened in intensity. Suddenly, the hillside before them seemed to open up and, exhausted, Hal dropped to the ground. The others stared in wonder at the passageway that had appeared from nowhere.

"You did it!" cried Tia in surprise.

Ben looked at Owen and Jacob and saw them smiling… it had been a long time since they had seen their families and they were looking forward to returning home.

Amy looked at Ben with tears in her eyes. "Are you sure you want to go back to Earthlingcragg?" she sobbed. "I thought you loved it here in Numblebrook."

"I do love it here, Amy, but I also love my family. They will have been at their wits' end wondering what has happened to me. I couldn't bear to never see them again."

"Will you return?" she cried, her heart laden with sadness.

"I don't know. Who knows what the future holds?" Ben hugged Amy and wiped away her tears. "I'll miss you every single day, and I'll never forget you," he sobbed.

"It has been a great honour to fight beside such a true friend!" Hal said as he patted Ben on the shoulder. "You are welcome back here any time you wish, Prince Benjamin Giddle, and I hope you will not forget us. We will never forget what you have done for this land, and we will forever be indebted to you." He turned to Owen and Jacob. "And you must also be proud of what you have achieved. You undertook some dangerous missions and have played your part in overthrowing King Ados. For that, we thank you."

The friends bade their farewells. Ben gave Shami a pat on her huge head and told her to take care of Amy. With tears in his eyes, he looked at his friends one more time and then turned to leave. As he did so, to his utter astonishment, he saw the dog with two tails strolling down the passageway towards them.

"Hurry up! My mistress is getting anxious; she doesn't like the passageway staying in the same place for too long. All this sentimental rubbish… there's absolutely no need for it. Get a move on!" The dog then turned around and started walking back down the passageway into the gloom.

"We had better hurry before the passage disappears!" exclaimed Jacob nervously.

As they walked down the tunnel into the darkness, they turned for one last time to wave goodbye to their friends. Ben felt a tear running down his cheek and quickly wiped it away.

With saddened, heavy hearts, Amy and the Moonbeamers watched their friends depart, and as they stared, the passageway slowly disappeared. Before them, once again, was the hillside, its grass waving gently in the wind.

The tunnel dimmed until they were almost walking in complete darkness. Eventually they saw light ahead and entered the large chamber. The sign bearing the name *LABYRINTH JUNCTION* still hung on the wall, and the old hag sat stirring her pot.

"You were a long time!" she moaned. "When I sent you on that errand to deliver the letter to Haligan Lexin, I didn't expect it to take you weeks!"

"We had to go on many dangerous missions to overthrow an evil king. It wasn't something that could be done quickly!" retorted Ben in defence.

"Excuses, excuses! That's all I hear from the youth of today!" She looked at Owen and Jacob. "And what excuses have you two got?" Owen opened his mouth to speak, but the old hag continued. "Don't bother replying, laddie, I don't want to hear it! Now off you go, get out of my sight before you get yourselves in more trouble! I presume you are going back to Earthlingcragg? Or do you want to enter one of the other lands and end up in more bother?"

"Yes, we're definitely going back to Earthlingcragg!" spluttered Jacob, as he hastily walked towards the steps in the middle of the cavern.

As Ben approached the stone stairway, he looked around at the walls, looking for the mathematical formulae which had helped him to solve the riddle. "Where's the formula for pi gone?" he asked the witch.

"I told you mathematics solves many of the world's problems, and I was right, wasn't I? But it's not needed now; it has served its purpose!"

Ben looked at the spot where the number for pi had been, and in its place noticed an engraved map bearing a cross.

"What's that for?" he asked.

"Only time will tell!" she muttered. "Now be off with you!"

Ben turned to look at her as he went down the stone steps and was sure he noticed a sly wink and a wry smile spread across her face.

The boys reached the beach and ran as fast as they could towards the small village in which they lived. They had agreed to keep the Junction and Numblebrook a secret; besides, who would believe them anyway?

Ben reached his house, excitedly pushing open the door, eager to see his family after so many weeks. "Mum, Mum, I'm home!" he cried.

His mother appeared from the kitchen door with a stern look on her face. "Where's the milk?" she asked.

"What milk? What are you talking about?" asked a puzzled Ben. "Haven't you been wondering where I've been all this time? I thought you would be overjoyed to see me!"

"Don't play games with me, Ben. Have you bought the milk or not?" she replied angrily.

"Errmmm… No!" Ben answered, feeling very confused.

"Well, I suggest you go back to the shop and get it, then! Honestly, Ben, I just don't know what's got into you lately. You've been acting strangely for weeks!"

Ben turned to go back through the front door, his mind spinning with hundreds of questions. Milk? What milk? What was she talking about? And how could he have been acting strangely for weeks? He'd been missing for weeks, and hadn't anybody been wondering where he was? He stood on the porch, trying to make some kind of sense out of the situation, when something caught his attention and he stared in disbelief. Surely this could not be real! Walking up the driveway towards him was somebody who looked exactly like Ben himself, and he was carrying a bottle of milk! Only it couldn't be himself, as he was stood right there outside his own front door! But the person walking towards him looked identical, and was even wearing his clothes!

"Who-who-who are you?" asked Ben in wonder.

The identical Ben carrying the milk stopped and stared with a stern look on his face. "You could have warned me that you were coming home!" he answered crossly as he placed the milk on the floor.

"What do you mean, I could have warned you?! I don't know who you are or how you got here. Who are you?"

"I was sent here to clone you, of course! The witch from the Junction sent me so that your family wouldn't get worried. Two weeks, she said! I did not expect you to be gone for nearly two months! And what thanks do I get? Nothing!"

With that outburst the clone immediately vanished, and in its place sat a ginger tabby cat. Ben stared in bewilderment at the strange feline.

"Well," said the cat, "do I get any thanks or not? It wasn't easy being you for seven weeks, you know! In fact some of it was particularly unbearable! I had to put up with your stupid brothers teasing me for a start. And school! I don't even know where to begin with school! Those boys in your class are idiots! And a maths and spelling test every Friday! I'm a cat, you know! Cats aren't supposed to sit exams!"

"You sat my maths and spellings tests?" asked Ben in utter astonishment.

"Of course I did! I did object, but that stupid teacher of yours threatened to put me in detention!"

"Well, I hope you got good marks!" replied Ben. "I always get one hundred per cent!"

"You must be joking!" snarled the cat. "I'm a cat! I can't do maths and spell words. Your marks have gone right down, and your teacher thinks you've gone insane! As do the rest of your family, by the way! I don't know what you thought you could expect. I tried my hardest and it wasn't easy pretending to be you. You should just be grateful I was here to cover for you, whilst you were on your missions to save the world! I would much rather have gone off on some great adventure in Numblebrook, but instead I was stuck here putting up with your brothers and going to school!"

Ben was wondering how to answer, when two other cats ran towards them up the driveway.

"Owen's home!" shouted a grey Persian cat with long, fluffy hair. "He gave me no notice whatsoever! Nearly got caught, I did! And no gratitude either!"

"Nor from Jacob!" chirped a black cat. "Still, I suppose this nightmare is now over. I was sick of going to that silly school. We better report back to the witch and see what other stupid mission she's going to send us on next. She could have warned us that they were on their way back!"

All three cats started to walk back down the driveway towards the road, chatting as they went. Ben stared after them in utter confusion.

"Oh, and one more thing," shouted back the tabby cat. "Tell that idiotic dog of yours, I chucked all his chews in the bin. He's been searching for them all week! It's not in my job description to be nice to dogs!"

Ben stared in disbelief as the cats disappeared from view. He shook his head and turned to walk into the house, utterly baffled at the situation he had just found himself in. He placed the milk on the kitchen worktop.

"At last!" his mother chirped.

Ben went up to his room, still confused about what had just happened. He lay on his bed and felt his eyes grow heavy… he was so tired after everything that had happened. Before he knew it, he was fast asleep, dreaming about all the strange things that had happened in the land of Numblebrook.

He woke to his mother shaking him gently, telling him that his tea was on the table. He ate slowly, deep in thought about his adventures and how unreal they now seemed. Had it all been a strange but realistic dream? The more he thought, the more this seemed like the only sensible answer. How could he have been fooled by such a silly dream?

He lay in bed that evening feeling both angry and sad; angry with himself for believing such adventures could happen, and sad that his friends must have been simply figments of his imagination. Whilst he was deep in thought, his mother walked into the room and put something down on his bedside cabinet.

"You've been collecting pebbles on the beach again! I wish you would empty your pockets before you put your clothes in the washing basket. It could damage the washing machine!"

As she walked from the room, Ben looked in disbelief at the stone she had placed on the cabinet… the moonstone! He quickly picked it up and started to rub it frantically, repeating Amy's name over and over again. At first nothing happened and Ben started to think that maybe it really was just a pebble from the beach. But then, slowly, it began to warm in his hands and tingle between his fingers. He stared at the stone in amazement as it became hazy, then slowly Amy's face began to appear.

"You took your time!" she laughed. "I thought you had forgotten all about me!"

A huge smile crossed Ben's face. "How could I possibly forget you and my adventures in Numblebrook?" He grinned. "How are things there since I left?"

"They're great. King Haligan is a strong and honourable king and the land is now the joyful and peaceful place it once was. Everybody is happy… apart from me, that is. It's just not the same here, not now that you are gone."

"Is there anything I can do?" asked Ben, guilt spiralling through him.

A large, mischievous grin appeared on Amy's face. "You could meet me at the Junction tomorrow?" she laughed. "I quite fancy the idea of visiting Smugglers' Way!"

An image of the engraved map etched into the cave wall of Labyrinth Junction sprang into Ben's mind. Smugglers' Way! Maybe it was a treasure map? After all, smugglers do steal treasure! Now wouldn't that make a great adventure? Ben grinned excitedly back at the image of Amy and nodded enthusiastically.

"Tomorrow it is, then!" he laughed.